Too Young to Be a *Grandma!*

*Thank you for being a friend!
Hope you enjoy!
Sandi Lorraine
S.*

Too Young to Be a Grandma!

SANDI LORRAINE

Copyright © 2015 by Sandi Lorraine.

Library of Congress Control Number: 2015911616
ISBN: Hardcover 978-1-5035-8764-9
       Softcover 978-1-5035-8766-3
       eBook   978-1-5035-8765-6

All rights reserved. No part of this book may be reproduced or transmitted in any form or by any means, electronic or mechanical, including photocopying, recording, or by any information storage and retrieval system, without permission in writing from the copyright owner.

This is a work of fiction. Names, characters, places and incidents either are the product of the author's imagination or are used fictitiously, and any resemblance to any actual persons, living or dead, events, or locales is entirely coincidental.

Any people depicted in stock imagery provided by Thinkstock are models, and such images are being used for illustrative purposes only.
Certain stock imagery © Thinkstock.

Print information available on the last page.

Rev. date: 07/22/2015

To order additional copies of this book, contact:
Xlibris
1-888-795-4274
www.Xlibris.com
Orders@Xlibris.com
696037

A special thank you
To my children
For making me
A grandmother,
And to my
Husband
For being a great
Grandfather.

CHAPTER ONE

"Grandma!" Danika Bronson repeated the word several times to herself as she walked to the corner of Sixth and Mulberry streets. Even though her mind was whirling the disgusting word around in her head, she automatically stopped with the rest of the crowd to wait for the green light to give them the go ahead to cross. The parking ramp was across the street and several blocks away so this little jaunt gave her more time to think about the package she had received in the mail yesterday from her only child, Jani.

Jani and her husband lived in Denver, Colorado, so Danika didn't get to see her as often as she would like. She hadn't heard from her daughter for over a month now, so when this package arrived by special delivery, Danika was excited to see what was in it. What could Jani possibly be sending her? It was mid-July, five months before Danika's birthday and Christmas, and those were the only times Jani ever sent her gifts and vise-versa.

It had taken her a couple of minutes to comprehend the meaning of the gift after opening it. And she hadn't been prepared for the blow! It was a pink satin baby blanket, with bright colored embroidering of baby rattles, pins, and teddy bears all over it, plus big, bold, rose colored lettering across it that said, "Baby girls are a gift from Heaven." There wasn't any letter or note to explain what it meant. Just the blanket and Danika was instantly upset. She had expected this to take place sooner or later, and she had always hoped it would be later, because she wasn't ready to be called, "Grandma!"

She did a quick calculation in her head. It had only been two years since Jani had gotten married, and Danika just knew that she couldn't possibly be ready to start having children. She just hoped Jani wasn't rushing things like she and Jani's dad had done, because after seventeen years of marriage, they had been divorced.

Jani had taken four years of college at Drake University to become a lawyer like her dad. That's where she and Rick had met. He had popped the question shortly after they had dated for a year and they were married a year later, before Jani graduated. Rick had already landed a good job as a computer programmer before they were married, so when he sent resumes out to the Denver area, he didn't have any problem finding a good job, and Jani had been fortunate enough to land a job with a high ranking criminal defense attorney. She hadn't been out of college long enough to fit into the working field, so how could she even think of working and juggling kids at her age?

Danika waited for the elevator to fill up before pushing the button to the fifth floor of the Beemer Building, where her elaborate office was. As she stepped into the suite occupied by her publishing firm, she stopped and just looked around, taking in the immenseness of it all. Cubicles were filled with employees of both genders and nationalities, ranging from ages twenty one to sixty five. She had worked long, hard, hours trying to build The Complex & Elaborate, a magazine that covered all kinds of stories, all over the United States, and now overseas, about people, places, and things that were both complex and elaborate. If only Rosetta Dunfee could see what she had accomplished now!

Danika had started her career as a journalist and free-lance writer working for the huge Meredith Corporation. It had always been a cut throat contest between her and Rosetta, a five foot, five inch, red headed, thirty year old, built like a Barbie doll with an abundance of energy, who had the best opportunity to cover the most attractive articles. Too many times Danika had been stuck with covering the lesser important articles at home because of her husband and later, a daughter. Rosetta had always gotten to do the overseas articles while Danika had always been stuck covering the articles closer to home so that she wasn't gone over night more than a couple of nights at a time. Rosetta had always made it her goal to elaborate on the fact that *she* had been picked to cover articles like royal weddings, newly released Paris fashions and anything else that she could hold over Danika's head. So eventually, Danika decided to break away and start her own magazine, covering what she enjoyed writing about. But, putting that goal ahead of her husband and daughter, had eventually led to the divorce and the loss of the two most precious things that really mattered in her life.

Her husband and his best friend's wife had struck up an affair with Danika asking for a divorce from him when she finally found out about it. The divorce was a bitter one, and what made it harder to swallow was the fact that Jani wanted to stay with her dad in the suburb of Johnston instead of moving to the inner city of Des Moines with her mother when the child custody battle landed before the judge. Jani had complained that her mother was always gone too much, plus she was involved in sports that she felt she wouldn't get to enjoy if she moved, so the judge granted Jani her wishes to remain with her dad.

Now Danika was about to turn forty three years old and become a grandmother at the same time, and she wasn't happy about it. Even though she had worked hard and had been under a lot of stress trying to build her own company, she had taken good care of herself by eating healthy foods, working out at the Gym at least three times a week, playing racquet ball with a couple of friends when she could, swimming at the YMCA, and going to a couple of the country clubs to play tennis or golf every chance she had. Not only did it help keep her in shape, but it kept her occupied and informed of all the latest gossip in the city so she could continuously find things to send her staff to check out for articles for the magazine, plus it helped take her mind off of the hurt she had felt and went through when she had been dumped for another woman.

"Good morning, Ma'am," Tara Dorsey smiled when Danika walked into her office. Tara was a petite brunette about thirty years old, stood five foot, three inches tall, married to a wonderful husband and had two small children. She was good at her job, and Danika depended immensely on her capabilities. To get to Danika, everyone had to get past Tara. No one got to talk to or see Danika without Tara "Okaying" it first.

Danika smiled and reached for the mail in her *incoming* basket. "Anything special I need to know about?" she asked.

"Well, you have a good looking man waiting for you in your office."

"Who?" Danika frowned. Who would be important enough for Tara to let into her office without Danika's permission first?

"It's your ex," Tara whispered.

"Ken?" Danika was shocked. She hadn't had any reason to talk to or see Ken since their daughter's wedding two years ago. "What could he possibly want today?"

Tara shrugged her shoulders. "I hope it was okay for me to let him wait in there."

"I guess we'll see!" Danika scowled. *Of all days, why did he have to upset it more by showing up?*

When he stood up as she entered the room, Danika's heart skipped a couple of beats. Dark haired, Kenneth Bronson, looked just as handsome and debonair today as he had twenty some years ago when Danika had married him. If anything, even more so because he was a six foot, well-developed hunk of a man now and not a scrawny, just graduating college kid. His mischievous blue eyes that she had always loved, combed over her, approving of what he was seeing and he didn't try hiding his feelings about what he felt.

"Wow! For a soon to be grandmother, you look great!" he grinned and skimmed his eyes over her again, making her feel conspicuous. And why the heat was burning her cheeks all of a sudden was beyond her comprehension. Could it be because of the way his eyes always sparkled when he teased her? Or was it because of the way she still felt about him? Or maybe it was because she just couldn't get used to good looking men complimenting her without feeling somewhat embarrassed? For some reason, she had developed a sense about not trusting any man that tried to make over her. Were they doing it to intimidate her, interested in her wealth, or because they actually thought she was a handsome woman? She could never be sure and she never gave them the benefit of the doubt. It was pertinent that she had to keep herself poised at all times if she was to compete in this man's cruel world of business competition.

"Hello, Ken." Danika wasn't smiling. "I take it you know about Jani's baby girl?"

"Isn't it great? I'm so excited about being a grandpa! I can't wait!"

"How long have you known?" Danika asked.

"I just found out yesterday when Jani sent me a package with a box of cigars in it that say 'I'm the proud grandpa of a baby girl' on the band. She said she thought I might enjoy handing them out at the office and the country club when the baby comes. I had to call her right away to tell her how excited I am for her and Rick."

"That's nice," Danika passed it off as she walked around her desk and sat down in her padded office chair.

"You've got yourself a pretty nice place here," Ken said, looking around. "It looks like you've done well for yourself."

Danika just smiled. How did she accept his compliment when down deep in her heart, she knew this nice place had cost her the man she loved?

"You've done pretty well yourself! Congratulations on your appointment of becoming District Attorney."

"Thanks!" Then Ken's smile turned serious. "How have you been?"

"I'm fine! And you?"

"You know that Sonya and I got a divorce over a year ago, don't you?" He sat back down in one of the chairs in front of her desk, crossing his long legs to get comfortable.

"I think I remember reading something about it in the gossip section of the daily paper. It must not have affected your election?" *How well she remembered seeing it in the paper. Now she had all she could do to contain all the questions she had swimming in the back of her head that wanted to escape her mouth as to what and why?*

"No," he shook his head. "I was worried there for a while when reporters kept bringing it up. I wasn't sure how the public would feel about it. But," he sucked in a deep breath, "we just couldn't get along. We tried, but it didn't work out. So I decided to take my chances with the election. If I won, Okay and if I didn't, Okay. I couldn't stand the fighting and bickering anymore."

Ordinarily Danika might have been sympathetic with someone telling her this. But, this time she felt like Sonya and Ken had gotten what they deserved for what they had put the two families through by having an affair. Sonya's husband had been so broken up about it that he started drinking heavily, and eventually took his own life by hanging himself in his garage. Sonya's son, who was a couple of years younger than Jani, had found his dad, and had started using and dealing drugs, and was now serving a five year prison term for it. Danika had turned bitter and plunged herself into building this magazine company, rejecting any advances or propositions by men in general.

"So," Ken changed the subject. "How did you find out about our new little bundle that's coming?"

Why did he have to be so excited about this? "I received a package with a pink baby blanket with the words, 'Baby girls are a gift from Heaven' written on it," she replied.

Ken laughed out loud and slapped his knee. "Doesn't that sound just like our Jani? Did she tell you when her due date is? I was so excited that I forgot to ask the exact date when I talked to her. She's going to email me a picture of the ultra sound scan. She probably sent you one, too. Have you checked?"

"I haven't had time to talk to her, yet," Danika admitted.

"How could you not just drop everything to call about such wonderful news?" Ken scowled.

"I—I've just been really busy this week. You know how it is when you have deadlines to meet," Danika lied. The truth was that she *wasn't* happy about it and didn't want to admit it to Ken! She thought of grandmothers as being eighty years old, plump, grey hair, sitting in a rocking chair, knitting or crocheting, just waiting for her kids and grandkids to come home to visit. Grandmothers *weren't* forty three years old, blond, trim and neat, professional business women that still looked sexy, with feelings and needs for the opposite sex.

"Well, I suppose I should head on to my office and let you get to work," Ken almost sounded like he hated to leave. He took his card case out of his suit pocket and handed her a business card. "Call me if you find out when her due date is. Maybe we can go out together and be there when the baby comes."

"You mean *be there* when she has it?" Danika frowned.

"Of course! Remember how excited our parents were when she was born?"

"No, not really!" Danika shook her head. "I just wanted to be left alone. I looked and felt like hell, but no one had enough sense to leave."

"Of course not," Ken acted surprised by her remark. "We were all so proud of you for the beautiful baby girl that you delivered and shared with us. Remember how much dark hair she had? The nurses were able to put a little bow in it."

Proud??? She had felt a lot of things that day, but being *proud* wasn't one of them. She could still remember the pain of the contractions and how they had kept telling her to push, push, push, when it hurt so bad, plus the way the nurses continued coming in and pushing on her tender stomach in front of everyone afterwards, checking her swollen and painful bottom after producing and forcing an eight and a half pound creature through a small opening the size of a pickle jar lid, and trying to squeeze the daylights out of her sore boobs to produce milk when she kept telling them that she didn't have the time or desire to nurse it every three to four hours,---which in in Jani's case turned into every two to three hours for the first four weeks of her life. And looking or feeling sexy for her husband, like she had always prided herself for being, was completely out of the question.

She had thought that Ken was going to have to act as a referee between the two sets of grandparents as each one wanted to be the first to hold their new grandchild. He had stepped in between them and told all four of them that *he* was going to be the very first. From there he handed the baby to his mother and then on to Danika's mom before the two grandfathers got a chance. Danika could still remember the hell she had gone through later from her mother, who had been extremely upset at the time and had constantly reminded her for several years afterward of how she had been cheated out of being the first to hold her very first grandchild.

"Kenny's parents already had a grandchild from his older sister," she had complained. "So why couldn't I have been the first to hold my first granddaughter?"

It hadn't made any difference how much Danika had tried soothing her mother's feathers, that episode at the hospital was one that she had never won out on, and Danika was sure that one of the reasons that her mother had upheld her throughout her and Ken's divorce was because her mother had never forgiven Ken for making her be third in line to hold the new baby.

"Funny! I never realized that all of you were so proud at the time," Danika scoffed. "I just remember our mothers acting like school age children fighting over a new play station, with each one wanting to be the first to have the controls to it."

"Well, if you didn't, you should have!" Ken frowned.

Danika stood up from her chair. "I really need to get busy," she started shuffling papers that sat in a pile in front of her. Ordinarily she would have stayed and worked on the pile the night before. But, after the package had arrived and she saw what was inside it, she was too upset to concentrate on going over the new articles before putting them together for the final layout. Not only that, but she wasn't interested in reminiscing about old times with Ken, whether they be good or bad.

Ken took the hint and stood up. Hesitating, he said, "I still miss you, Dani. Do you suppose we could get together for lunch sometime soon?"

It took Danika by surprise. After all the pain and embarrassment he had put her through, and now he wanted recourse? As usual, she blurted out the first thing that crossed her tongue, without weighing it first in her mind. "Well, I don't miss you," she lied. With that she handed him back his business card and said, "You can hand this to Tara on your way out. She'll see to it that it gets filed with all the rest."

"But...!" Ken started, but stopped. "That's right! You don't need to carry this card with you so you can call me. I had forgotten that you eat, sleep, and live this place, don't you? You don't need anybody! I'm surprised you don't have a bed set up in here since it means so much to you." His voice cracked like ice.

Danika gave him a smirking smile. "That's what that plush davenport is for. Now if you'll excuse me, I have work to do!"

"Same old Danika! Your daughter will always have to play second fiddle to your own whims, won't she? It was bad enough that I always had to, but Jani didn't deserve it." With those heated words, Ken snatched the card from her fingers and stalked out of her office, ignoring Tara as he walked past her desk.

Danika sank back down in her chair. With elbows propped on her desk, she buried her face in her hands, hoping she could keep the tears from erupting. Ken's last statement had stung just as hard as if he had taken a whip to her. As much as she didn't want to admit it to even herself, she knew he was speaking the truth. She had let herself get so wrapped up in trying to build this magazine company that she had lost the two things that mattered the most in her life. Now she was paying the consequences of it. She had the magazine, had plenty of wealth, had won several recognition awards, but didn't have anyone to share it with or wrap her arms around when the day was over. How she missed that.

She thought back to when Jani was born and after they had brought her home. Ken would take his turn at feeding and changing her, plus so many times he would take her out of her crib when she was sleeping and carry her around, admiring her. "Isn't she just the most precious thing?" he would say.

When Jani was growing up, she was involved in softball and basketball and he never missed one of her games. Time and time again, Danika had been busy with covering news articles or trying to meet deadlines, and missed them, always to come home to a heart broken daughter that didn't understand, and an upset husband.

"Ma'am," Tara's voice flowing through the intercom of her speaker phone interrupted her self-pitying innuendos.

"Yes."

"Josh is ready to do the layout and was wondering if you've finished with everything?"

"I haven't gotten through it all, but tell him to come and get it anyway, because I don't have time to mess with it today."

"Are you sure?" Tara's voice sounded surprised. This was so unlike Danika. "You don't have any appointments until two this afternoon."

"Yes! I'm sure." Danika answered.

"Don't you feel well?"

"No. Not really. In fact, would you please cancel those two appointments for this afternoon and re-schedule them. I think I'm going to go back home for a while."

"Yes Ma'am. I hope you get to feeling better."

"I'm sure I will. I just need to get rid of this headache. You can call me if anything serious comes up."

"Okay."

Danika could hear the concern in Tara's voice. This was not like Danika, either. Many times she had come to work with a headache, running a fever, or the sniffles, to name a few, but she just never stayed home from work. She had a job to be done and only she could make it happen.

CHAPTER TWO

As soon as Danika reached her apartment, she poured herself a tall glass of Yellow Tail Merlot and sat down in front of her computer. She might as well get this over with because a short goblet of the relaxing wine wasn't going to do the trick today. She decided against skyping Jani. She didn't want her daughter to be able to see how she was feeling right now. First she checked her emails, and sure enough, there was the ultra sound picture of Jani's baby. It was still small enough that Danika had to study it at every angle to know just exactly what it was that she was looking at. How they knew yet that it was a girl, was beyond all of her reasoning power. How could anybody be excited about something that was still ugly and undistinguishable? All she could understand was the baby's head, legs, and arms. She inhaled a deep breath, shut the computer off and picked up her phone so she could call Jani. She always used her land line phone or skyped when she called her daughter, because she didn't want to tie up her cell phone in case her office needed to get ahold of her for some reason.

"Mom?" Jani answered in an excited tone of voice. "Did you get your package?"

Danika cleared her throat and tried to instill a cheerful voice to match her daughter's. "Yes!"

"Did you get your email of the ultra sound?"

"Yes. I received it too."

"Isn't she beautiful?" Jani crooned.

Beautiful? How did you tell your only daughter that *her* daughter was anything but beautiful right now? How could she lie herself out of this one?

"I'm sure she looks just like my beautiful daughter did at that stage," she replied. "How far along are you?"

"Four months! Now do you want to hear the best news?"

Sure, why not! What she had seen and heard so far was everything but good news.

"Yes! By all means, tell me your good news!"

"She is due to arrive two days before your birthday! Wouldn't it be great if she was born *on* your birthday?"

"Damn!" Danika choked on the sip of wine she had just taken, spewing wine all over her desk and her pink Armani suit.

"Mom! Are you okay? What's wrong?"

"I just accidently bumped my glass of wine and spilled it all over the desk and my suit," she lied.

"I'm sorry! Do you want to call me back after you've got it all cleaned up? You better get something on that suit right away or it will stain it."

"Yes…! Yes! Maybe I had better do that! It will take me a while, but I will call you back later." With that, Danika hung the phone back on the receiver cradle and exhaled another deep breath. She hurried to the bathroom and tried to wipe the wine spots off of her skirt with a wet wash cloth, hoping the red juice didn't stain it beyond being wearable after being dry cleaned. Thank goodness her laptop computer had been closed so the wine hadn't gotten on the keyboard. What a mess that would have been to add to the already messed up day.

After working with no avail to get the wine spots off of her skirt, Danika slipped into a pair of silk lounging pajamas and refilled her wine glass. Instead of going back to talking to Jani, she curled up on her couch and picked up the latest edition of People Magazine and thumbed through it. Usually she read it from stem to stern, but today, there wasn't one article in it that interested her. Her mind kept going back to Ken and him telling her that he still missed her.

"Why?" she mumbled out loud. Why did he have to show back up in her life today? It had taken her years to get completely over him. And now, finally when she could have at least one or two weeks without thinking about him and the past, he shows up looking better than ever to her. She could still smell his after shave or cologne. He was still wearing men's Stetson. He had always worn it while they were dating, and evidently still liked it. Damn! So did she! He should be able to afford something more exotic now, so why was he still buying cheaper cologne that you could purchase in every Walmart and K-Mart? Was he paying alimony to Sonya?

She remembered the hassle they had went through when they had gotten their divorce. Not only did his lawyer try to get her to pay alimony to Ken, but for all of Jani's child support, including insurance and college tuition. She didn't mind paying for all of Jani's care and tuition, since her income exceeded far more than Ken's at the time and she assumed still did. In fact, she had paid for all of Jani and Ricks wedding expenses. All Ken had to do was pick up his tuxedo and walk Jani down the aisle. But paying the son-of-a-bitch alimony was completely out of the question. He was the one doing the cheating. His new wife could find a job just like she had to do all of their married life. He had condemned her for working so hard and claimed infidelity, yet he had the gall to ask for some of that hard earned income to support his new wife with.

She downed another long swig of the Merlot. Just thinking of the past had her mind whirling again. How could she still miss him and find him attractive when he had put her through so much heartache? Not only how, but why?

He had forgotten how good looking and sexy looking his ex-wife was until she walked into her office. Her long, two toned blond, wavy hair still had a shine to it and she hadn't gained one pound since their divorce. She still had a Barbie Doll figure that he had never grown tired of looking at and appreciating. He remembered how the men in his office drooled over her every time she stopped in to see him. "Wow, you have to be the luckiest man there is to have a stacked wife like her. I bet she's hot in bed," they would tease.

At the time, he had to admit that she was. But the problem was, she wasn't in bed often enough to satisfy his needs. She was always chasing off getting another news report for that damned magazine company.

But today, sitting in her office and seeing her, stirred up that old feeling of arousal again. A feeling he hadn't been prepared for. And when those turquoise blue eyes of hers had teased about the plush davenport in her office, he actually found himself feeling jealous, thinking and wondering how many men she had made love to on that comfy piece of furniture. After all, she worked many nights in her office by herself. Or so she had always said, and so many times he had a hard time believing her, even though she had never actually given him any proof to mistrust her.

And now, after he had tossed her away for something he thought was there to keep him satisfied, he knew that not only had Sonya been having an affair with him, but also another country club member. She had only married him to get away from her husband. And because he was a lawyer, she had assumed he had the money to support her expensive habits, which he didn't. It hadn't taken very long for him to realize that he had made a terrible mistake. But, pride kept him from admitting it to anyone. He had put up with Sonya's cheating and expensive traits,--which she wasn't willing to help contribute the dollars too,--longer than most men would have. It was bad enough when he had to let Danika pay for all of Jani's wedding because he was too broke to help foot the bill, but the last straw was when he discovered Sonya had emptied out their checking account and borrowed the limit against all their credit cards to bail her son out of jail when he had been charged for manufacturing, transporting and dealing in methamphetamine and cocaine. Several times her son had been bailed out and had served six weeks or so in the county jail. But now after the third charge for the same thing, he was serving five years in the state pen in Fort Dodge.

Ken was still paying the price, as long overdue bills that Sonya had racked up with her elaborate spending, were still popping up. Because Ken didn't want his name to be involved in civil courts for owing money to people, he had been struggling to pay them off.

And to think the woman had the gall to fight for alimony from him. Thank goodness, he knew who the best lawyer in town was to handle such affairs, and he was sure that belonging to the Wakonda country club and playing golf with the judge hadn't hurt anything, either.

Danika finished cleaning the sticky wine off her desk, and then curled back up on the davenport with her third glass of Yellow Tail, before calling Jani back. But first, she made an addition to the grocery list to buy more Yellow Tail. She was also out of lettuce, pretzel bread, blue cheese crumbles, cream cheese, celery, and peanut butter. When all else failed to satisfy her hunger when she was burning the late night lamp light, celery sticks with peanut butter or cream cheese filling always did the trick.

Danika's conversation with Jani was much more tolerable the second time around, thanks to the three glasses of wine. If Jani noticed a change in her attitude, she didn't mention it. In fact, Danika let Jani ramble on about what they wanted to name the baby and what they had already purchased and what they still needed. Danika let her do all the talking and just agreed if she realized that Jani was asking a question or just showing her excitement. The only time she disagreed with anything was when Jani mentioned that she would appreciate it if her mother would come and stay for a couple of weeks when the new little addition came.

"How long I get to stay will depend on how close to closing edition time your baby comes," Danika said. When she heard the disappointment in Jani's voice she stated, "However, if I can't make it, your father is planning on coming to stay with you and he was great at changing *your* diapers." Jani laughed and replied, "I can't wait to see how well Rick handles her."

And then Jani said something else that struck Danika wrong!

"Guess what Mom? We've been looking at houses and trying to decide if we want to buy a two or three bedroom home. I didn't realize how much owning a home of your own cost until we started looking.

But our apartment is only a one bedroom, so before the baby comes, we have to find something so she will have her own room."

"Don't you think your apartment can suffice until you get back on your feet a little bit more? Are you planning on going back to work after the baby comes?"

"I haven't decided yet," Jani answered, sounding a bit disappointed by her mother's lack of enthusiasm like she was feeling.

"Well, you are rushing things a bit," Danika scolded. "You should have thought about that *before* you decided to get pregnant. You seem to be getting the cart ahead of the horse!"

Danika knew the minute she felt Jani's hesitation and then a quick "goodbye" following, that she had just spoken out of turn. It wasn't her life to lead, it was Jani's. So why was she so critical? Didn't she want her daughter happy?

She hung up from talking to Jani and then pulled the phone book out of the top desk drawer to find Ken's office phone number. *Now* she wished she hadn't been such a snob and had kept his card. She probably had his cell phone number somewhere, but she had erased it off her phone long ago and didn't find it necessary to add when she updated and purchased a new phone. As soon as Jani had gotten married, she assumed that they would no longer have any reason to get in contact with each other, so not only had she deleted it from the contact list on her phone, but also her address list on the computer.

When she found his office number, she was informed by his office assistant that he was in a meeting and wouldn't be available until noon.

"Would you like to leave your name and a message?" the young, sweet voice asked.

"Just tell him that our baby is due December twenty third. He will know who is calling," Danika replied.

"Excuse me?" His secretary choked.

"You heard me right! I didn't stutter!" Danika hung up. At least now he couldn't accuse her of putting Jani in second place in her life!

CHAPTER THREE

Danika had just hung up from calling her office and discussing the next month's article layouts with Josh so it could be sent to printing, when a loud knock on the door startled her. Who on earth knew that she was home? It had to be a solicitor. But the apartment building had strict rules posted about solicitors entering the building. Besides that, no one had buzzed for her to open the main entrance door. She peered through the peep hole in the door and was even more shocked at the figure standing outside her door.

Ken thrust a bouquet of mixed flowers consisting of daisies, lilies, carnations, sunflowers, and baby's breath at her when Danika opened the door.

"What's this?" she scowled.

"A peace offering for the rude remark I made in your office. I know you like daisies and lilies. Don't be so skeptical," he added when she continued to just stand there frowning at him. Then he handed her a white sack. "Have you eaten yet?"

"I don't feel much like eating," she mumbled. "How did you know I was here, and how did you get in?"

"You have a great secretary," he continued to grin. "When I called to talk to you, she said you had come home because you have a horrible headache. But, I know you well enough to know that a headache of any caliber wouldn't send you home. So she gave me your address, made me promise she wouldn't get into trouble for telling me, and here I am." His sparkling deep blue eyes combed over her as he stepped past her and walked into her lavish apartment.

"Wow! You sure know how to live, don't you?" he asked as he looked around the room at the expensive contemporary furniture from Redeker's that it was furnished with. "Did you design and decorate everything yourself?"

"No! I had an interior decorator come in and do it," Danika answered. "I don't have time to fool with something like that."

"You did a good job with our house," he continued.

"How did you get to my door?" Danika changed the subject. "I didn't let you in."

"A nice little old lady that lives in this building was coming out just as I was getting ready to ring the buzzer. She was even nice enough to tell me which apartment was yours. I told her I was your brother and had flown all the way here from Chicago to surprise you."

Danika shook her head and rolled her eyes. That was scary! "It's a surprise alright!" she agreed.

"So do you want to eat at your kitchen table, the dining room or right here in your living room?" He reached in his bulging suit pocket and pulled out a bottle of blackberry wine. "Santa Maria vineyard," he grinned as he held it up for her to see. "Grown and brewed right here in Carroll County Iowa."

"And what's on the menu?" she finally managed a weak smile.

"Well, if my memory serves me right, you like cashew chicken from The Great China Buffet. Am I right?"

"You remembered right. So what are you eating?"

"I brought Mongolian Beef for me, plus cream cheese filled Rangoon's."

"Well, I guess the kitchen table should do the trick. I wouldn't want you to go to all of this trouble for nothing." She didn't add that she thought she had already drunk her quota of wine for the day. She knew this by the way the floor kept swaying under her feet as she led the way to the kitchen.

"I got your message," he stated as he followed behind her. "My secretary thought it was a prank call and wasn't sure about passing it on to me. She was afraid to ask me if I was expecting a baby," he laughed a shaky laugh. "I'm glad you called. Thanks."

Danika rummaged for a crystal vase in the hall closet to put the flowers in, filled the vase with water and proceeded to the formal dining room where she set the flowers in the center of the long dining room table on a doily. Then she strolled to the kitchen where Ken was pulling white rice boxes and Styrofoam plates out of the sack he had been carrying and placing on the table. She handed him two stoneware plates for the food, and a couple of goblets for the wine, out of the cupboard. "Do you want forks or do you still eat with chop sticks?"

"I'm fine with chop sticks," he replied as he pulled a chair out for her and then seated himself at the small kitchen table. Everything in the apartment was large and expensive, but since she was the only one to set at her table, she had just purchased a small set with two chairs. Most of the time she just drank her coffee and ate her morning bagel and yogurt sitting on one of the stools at the island bar; therefore, the table hardly ever got used. Very rarely did she eat other meals at home. Eating alone was no fun, so she usually ate at one of the clubs where there was always someone to talk to. Every Friday noon she paid to have sandwiches delivered to all of her employees from the Quizno's shop located on the same block as her office. Even though she tried to keep lettuce on hand at home so she could have a salad in the probability that she should eat alone, most of the time she ended up throwing it out due to spoilage before she got to eat it.

"I was afraid it would be cold by the time I got here," Ken said as he slid the box of cashew chicken over in front of her. "But, it still feels warm."

This was the first decent tone of conversation they had held between them since she had found out about him and Sonya's affair. They hadn't even been able to speak to each other with a civil tongue during Jani's graduation from high school, college, and then her wedding. And now as Danika thought about it, it hadn't necessarily been Ken that had the spiked tongue. It was always her. And the fact that he had the audacity to bring Sonya to all of Jani's special affairs that Danika had paid the bills for hadn't helped any of the situations either. But, Danika would always be grateful that she had the pleasure of helping Jani make all of her wedding decisions without Sonya sticking her nose into it like she had tried doing for Jani's high school and college graduation receptions. However, Sonya had administered a long list of friends to be invited to each affair that Danika knew damned well were her own personal acquaintances and not Kens that she wanted to make an impression on. But since Sonya was all about show, she wanted everyone on that list to think that she and Ken were paying for everything elaborate. Danika swore the dress Sonya had worn to Jani's wedding was twice as expensive as Jani's wedding dress. She had even bragged about going to New York to have it personally made just for her. Danika remembered how she just wanted to gag each time she had heard Sonya carrying on about it that eventful day. And to make things even worse, she had to stand in the same group setting with Ken and Sonya to have pictures taken.

"Did you tell my secretary that our baby is due on Christmas?" Ken asked as he dumped the rice on his plate, followed by the Mongolian Beef on top. "Possibly on your birthday! That is really neat!" He grinned when she nodded her head. "You should feel honored and special."

The fact that he remembered her birthday after all these years was an absolute miracle and caught her completely off guard. Danika took another long swallow of the blackberry wine, which really hit the spot. But, feeling *honored or special* wasn't the word for how she felt about the whole ordeal. Disgusted, revolting, repugnant, to name a few choice words, was more like it. And contrary to what Ken thought, being born a couple of days before Christmas was not a blessing. She had always felt cheated out of either getting a birthday gift or getting a Christmas gift. She was never sure which one it would have been. Her mother had always tried to console her by saying, "you don't know how lucky you are! You always get a much more expensive gift than if it was for two separate occasions." Danika had never known just how to feel and now her new granddaughter would probably feel just as confused about it as she always had!

"It would even make it all the more special if they named her after you. Did she tell you what names they have picked out?"

Danika shook her head, which was a mistake, because when she did, the room started swirling around her. Maybe Jani had. It seemed like she did, but Danika couldn't remember.

"I can't wait to tell the girls in my office that my first granddaughter could be born on Christmas day or could possibly be born on my wife's birthday and might even be named after her."

"First, let's get one thing... no two things... straight." Danika held up three fingers and then switched it to two when she realized Ken was staring at her hand. "First... I'm not your granddaughter and two... Jani isn't going to have your wife on my birthday. And two...or is that three...? She's not going to name it after me, and God forbid it be on Christmas day!"

A big enigmatic smirk streaked across Ken's face. "And have you drunk that whole bottle of Yellow Tail this morning since you came home?" He pointed to the empty bottle sitting on the counter.

"Maybe! And if I did?"

"When did you start drinking like this?"

"Like what?"

"When did you become an alcoholic?" he started scowling.

"I'm not an alcoholic!" Danika retorted.

"Are you sure?"

"Of course I'm sure!" Danika argued. "I know, because I don't have to attend those AAA meetings. Only alcoholics do!"

"You were late getting to work this morning, and you came home with a hangover headache. Have you been doing that a lot lately?"

"Absolutely not!"

"You never leave work to come home with a headache. So don't try lying to me. I know you better."

"You don't know me at all!" Danika reputed.

Ken arched his eyebrows, and said, "I know that the Danika I married would never be inebriated like this."

"Well, thank God, you aren't married to me now, are you?"

He shook his head in a sympathetic way. "Maybe it was a mistake for me to come here today."

"Yep!" She started to shake her finger, but stopped because watching the movement of it going back and forth made her eyes hurt.

"It was probably a big mistake alright! I'm sure you have some good looking female somewhere just wondering where you are and why you aren't eating lunch with her at some fancy restaurant."

"Well, just for your information, I don't have any good looking female sitting in a fancy restaurant wondering about me. I haven't dated anyone since Sonya and I got our divorce."

"Ah-hah! Since you got your divorce?" Danika shook her finger at him again. "That must mean that you were doing the same thing to her that you did me. You were dating someone else *before* you got your divorce. Naughty, naughty! Shame on you!"

"No!" he frowned. "That's not what I mean, and that's not what happened."

"So, what happened?"

"*She* was dating someone else while we were married."

"Couldn't you keep her satisfied?" Danika snickered.

He didn't answer. Instead, he took a large bite of rice and beef.

"You know they make Ci…Ci…alis and Vi….Viagra. I think that's what it's called…, for men these days that have problems with that. Their companies usually run full page ads in my magazine.

His face turned red. "I don't have a problem, and I don't need Viagra!"

"Hmmmm!" An evil grin swept across her face. "Are you sure? When's the last time you had sex?"

"Why?"

"Maybe you need it and you just don't want to admit it."

"I think it's time for me to leave. I've never seen you like this."

"What do you expect? You haven't actually *seen* me for sixteen years."

"No! And I've missed you! And right now, if you weren't drunk, I would try my best to *see* you and show you that I *don't* need Cialis or Viagra. You look mighty inviting in those sexy pajamas."

His comment took Danika completely off guard, and she finished the last swallow of her blackberry wine. "That's good wine," she mumbled. And then she said, "Grandmas and grandpas don't have sex."

Ken started laughing. "Is that your problem with the news of Jani's baby? You think by her having a baby that it will eliminate you from having sex?"

"No!" Danika frowned. "Well, maybe!" she admitted.

"So are you engaged in having sex with someone, and you're afraid you'll have to give it up if you become a grandma?"

"No! And if I was, I wouldn't tell you. You gave up caring about whether I was having sex or not, a long time ago."

She wasn't about to tell him that the only intercourse she had experienced since their divorce was a three month fling she had encountered with her French Masseur way back when.

Danika and Marla Crawford, Felicia Ferrell, and Alma Humphry, had all worked together for the Meredith Corporation in their earlier days, and because they seemed to have so much in common, like enjoying the same movies, the same books, golf, the same restaurants, they had eventually become best friends. Now everyone, except Alma, had moved on to something else to do with their lives. Danika had pursued a business of her own; Marla was about the same age as Danica; had married later in life; had two sons that were now teenagers, and worked out of her home as a free-lance reporter for Riemann Publishing Company out of Ames. Because her husband was a professor of biology at Iowa State University, they owned a fairly new elaborate home in a new housing area off of Highway #30 west of Ames. Felicia was about four years younger than Danika and had married into money and no longer had to work, so she become a stay at home mom after her two little girls came along, and now she kept busy in the PTA, Booster club, and volunteered three days a week to help at one of the preschools in West Des Moines. Alma was about four years older than Danika, and had worked herself up to be one of the senior editors at Meredith. She and her husband didn't have any children. Her husband was an insurance broker, and they lived in the older part of Des Moines on Woodlawn Ave, in a fabulous house that was filled with Victorian furniture. Also, they owned a condo on the beautiful Lake Panorama that was furnished with up to date contemporary attire.

The four of them continued to get together once a month to go to a movie, play golf, just go shopping, cuss and discuss Rosetta Dunfee's articles that she still obtained for the Meredith Corporation's magazines, or just whatever suited them. Since their husbands all belonged to separate country clubs, the women would get together once a week at one of the different clubs to eat lunch, depending on whose turn it was to host the get together, or at one of the more elite restaurants in town. Danika just happened to belong to three different clubs in the Des Moines area, so they never lacked for a place to get together.

Once, shortly after Danika's divorce, when they were all together, Danika had developed a horrible headache and it showed in her eyes how she was suffering.

"I know just the thing for you," Marla had snickered. "You need a massage by a real masseur. They know how to get the kinks out of your spine and relax those muscles."

"Yes!" Alma agreed. "And I know just the one for you to see."

"I don't need a massage therapist," Danika had contradicted. "I just need to go home, drink a glass of wine, take a hot shower, and stretch out in bed."

"Do you know a good therapist?" Felicia had asked. "Sometimes my husband comes home with a headache and hurts across his shoulders from sitting at a computer all day." And then her cheeks turned pink and she added, "Usually though, I can massage him enough that he forgets about his troubles."

"Ahhhh!" They all laughed and Marla pointed at Felicia's face and said, "You are blushing! That tells me that it probably goes from a massage to something else that makes him forget his headache. Doesn't it?" And Felicia blushed that much more and grinned, without giving Marla an answer.

"I know what!" Marla spoke up again. "Next month when we get together, why don't we *all* go see your therapist, Alma? I'm sure we could *all* use a good massage! Maybe Felicia can even learn a few more tips on how she can *massage* Sean even better than she does already!" And once more Felicia's face turned every shade of red as Marla put emphasis on the *massage* part. "Is it a male or female?"

"I've never been there, but I have a friend that goes all the time and that's all she talks about. She says he is a real French Masseur and when he is done with her she is so relaxed that she hates to leave."

"Ooooooh!" Marla crooned. "That even sounds better than before. A real Frenchman, huh?"

"Yes," Alma grinned. "And she says he has helped her sex life tremendously. She's not so knotted up now and has become more responsive when her husband starts petting."

"Ooooooh!" Marla exclaimed again. "Let's not wait until next month! Let's go sometime this month. I can't wait to see what he can do for me!"

Danika just laughed. "Well, I don't have a husband to go home to, so I don't need to get my sex life hyped up."

"Oh, come on!" Marla scolded. "Don't be such a stick in the mud. Who knows, maybe it will help you find another husband, or at least someone to cuddle up to besides the teddy bear that you won at the State fair."

So starting once a month, the women went together to get their massages by the Frenchman. It cost three hundred dollars a pop for each of them, but they all felt that it was worth it, especially since he was such a good looking hunk of a man that was at least three years younger than Danika and Marla, and he knew how to use his fingers to relax every muscle in their bodies. Well, *almost* every muscle. His salon was a quiet, serene place and instead of regular ceiling lights in the room where he worked his magic fingers on them, he used scented candle light and herbal oils such as lavender, mint, and chamomile on their skin. Off to the side of the salon, he had a hot tub and a spa. And while one of the women was being massaged, the other three had a choice of drinking a glass of French Pinot Noir in the hot tub or in the spa. Life was good!

At least for all of them except Danika! After six months of massages, it hadn't found her another husband *or* a bed mate to cuddle with.

And then after a nerve wracking week at the office, due to equipment breaking down, appointments being cancelled and rescheduled, and employees going on strike because some wanted the union in the place, and some didn't, Danika had a horrible headache that wouldn't go away, even with the help of Yellow Tail, Extra strength Tylenol, and hot showers. So she had Tara call and make her a special appointment with the Frenchman.

"He says to tell you that he can see you after hours today, if you don't mind coming in about six o'clock," Tara told Danika.

"I'll take it!" Danika replied. She was desperate for some relief.

"He says it will cost you extra, since it is after office hours." Tara spoke again.

"That's okay. I figured as much." Everything these days seemed to cost more if it wasn't during a nine-to-five schedule, and Monday through Friday noon.

Danika arrived right on time and Juan's broad shouldered, muscular body frame met her at the door. Danika got goose bumps every time she laid eyes on him. He had dark hair, dark brown eyes, always had a five o'clock stubble across his face, stood about five foot, eleven inches, and there wasn't an ounce of fat on him anywhere to be seen. Under the skin tight spandex gym clothes that he wore, his whole body reeked with muscularity, bulging biceps, taunt butt…and ohhhhh wow! One could only guess what lay in the bulging jock strap underneath the shorts.

"Would you like to get in the hot tub for a while before we get started," he asked. "And maybe enjoy a glass of wine or two to help you relax?"

It all sounded good to Danika so she nodded her head in agreement. But then she had a second thought zip through her head, and it wasn't a good one!

"Oh no!" she exclaimed. "Since I wasn't even thinking about coming here today, I don't have my regular workout clothes. And I hurried here from work just so I wouldn't miss my appointment."

Usually, the women changed from their street clothes into their bikini bathing suits for a workout, so they could get in the hot tub and spa and then give him as much access to their bodies as he possibly dared.

"Never mind, I have an extra pair of gym shorts you can wear," Juan replied.

"That would be great! Do you mind?"

Juan shook his head and disappeared into his office only to reappear carrying only a pair of his spandex gym shorts for her to put on.

"What about a bra or a T-shirt?" she asked, when he handed them over to her.

"You'll be fine," he smiled. "There isn't anyone here except you and me, and I won't tell, if you don't. Besides, you'll be lying face down on the table, so you won't be exposing anything." He had always insisted that the women wear bikini tops that tied in the back so he could untie and retie when he massaged their backs.

"And for me to get from the dressing room to the hot tub and then on to the table, what will I do?"

"You can always wrap a towel around yourself, because I won't see you once you are in the tub."

Danika guessed he was right, so she took the gym shorts and hurried to the dressing room to strip off her suit and underclothes. When she emerged from the dressing room, she had a towel wrapped around her like he had suggested, but she caught the ardent smile he gave her as he watched her make her way to the hot tub. And when she caught it, it made every one of her hormones come to life and swarm into high gear like bees buzzing, letting her know that even after all that she had been through, she could still feel like a whimsical female. She turned her back towards him and gingerly dropped the towel and stepped into the tub, sinking her whole body beneath the whirl pooling water. It felt awesome so she leaned her head back against the edge, let the whirlpool float her feet to the top, and shut her eyes, just soaking in the pleasure of it.

"Do you want a glass of wine?" Juan's voice was right beside her ear, bringing her upright with a jolt. She instantly crossed her arms over her breast so that he couldn't see the effect he had upon her, and how her firm nipples were now protruding straight out in the clear water. He handed her a large goblet filled with wine, and with eyes twinkling, watched the turmoil she was in when she took her hand *away* from her breast to reach for the goblet. But then she remembered that if she took the goblet, he would see all of her nude upper half through the clear bubbling water. But if she didn't reach for the goblet, she couldn't drink the wine that she knew she desperately needed to help her relax.

"Just set it there on the edge and I'll help myself later," she instructed.

"Sure," he glanced at his watch. "But just remember, my price doubles after seven o'clock."

"So would you mind looking somewhere else while I drink my wine, and then I promise I'll be right there for my massage?"

"Okay!" He pursed his lips and turned and walked away. She quickly swallowed down the wine, as she watched him light more candles and set his bottles of herbal oils out on a little rolling stand that he placed beside the massage table. She wasn't about to pay him $600 for a treatment tonight, headache or no headache. As soon as the wine was gone, she covered her breasts once more with her crisscrossed arms, climbed out of the heavenly hot tub,--making a mental note in the back of her mind that she was going to have a Jacuzzi installed in her apartment,—wrapped a towel around her and hurried to where he stood waiting for her.

Opening the towel just enough so she could lay face down on the table without him seeing all of her from the waist up, she stretched out on her stomach and relaxed, anticipating the pleasure of the massage. She felt him pour the warm oils on her back and very gently begin to rub her back in a circular motion. First he worked up around her shoulders, and then all the way down to her waistband. But then, he asked her to extend her arms toward the top of her head, so that he could work the shoulder blades better to get the teneseness out of them. It didn't make sense to her, but she did as she was instructed. And then once more, he gently glided his hands farther on down her back, pressing on every muscle that she had. Then slowly, he kneaded his way back up to the middle of her back, letting his hands work completely around her rib cage, until he gently bumped both of her breasts that were peeking out from under her.

She felt it and it sent jolts throughout her whole being, making those hormone bees buzz that much more. Thinking that maybe it had been an accident, she didn't scold, or say anything. He continued to massage with his hands across her back, up and down, from neck to waist, and just when she was completely relaxed and thoroughly enjoying this extended massage, his hands slid around her rib cage again and this time he stoked both of her breasts. When she quickly inhaled a deep breath, he stopped with the back and dribbled oil down the backs of both of her legs. He began massaging the legs, starting with the bare toes and working his way up. This was a whole new ball game for Danika. It was something he had never done when the four women were there together. And, Oh wow! She couldn't believe the effect that it was having on her.

"Such lovely feet you have, Madame," he stated.

Lovely feet? Who had ever heard of lovely feet? Danika wondered.

"Your feet show wonderful love lines," once more he stated.

Danika had never heard of feet having love lines. Hands…yes! But feet?? No!

"Your feet show that you must have a wonderful sex life, Madame."

Danika snorted out loud. "Me? A wonderful sex life?" she laughed. "Who are you trying to kid?"

"I'm not trying to be funny," he said as his thumbs continued to press special spots on the bottom of her feet.

She felt an undeniable ache surge through her groin and up her spine. By the time he left her feet and had worked his way up to the hemline of the gym shorts, she was struggling to keep her mouth shut. She had the most uncontrollable urge to tell him to take them off so he could keep right on massaging. She gritted her teeth---not in anger, but in the agony of forcing self-control. And then his fingers stretched beyond the hem to the cheeks of her buttocks and all-most touched that sensitive place that was now crying out for him to cop a feel. She had all she could do to keep from flipping herself over, just so he could easily access what he was feeling.

Then he did the most unbelievable thing. He crawled up on the table with her and straddled her body with his knees. He leaned down and kissed her first on one of her shoulders, and then on the back of her neck, and then started nibbling on one of her ear lobes at the same time that his fingers continued to search under the tight spandex that was hugging her body too tight.

"What...?"

"Turn over," he whispered in her ear.

".....are you doing?"

"The massage is over," he whispered. "I can't believe you aren't having a good sex life. There has to be something wrong if you aren't."

"But..!"

He started nuzzling her ear again and planting tender kisses on the back of her neck while his fingers finally found what they were searching for and began to tease, taking her breath away. Those female hormones had suddenly been fueled like pouring a tanker of kerosene on a fast raging forest fire and she lost all common fear of being burned.

He took his time building her up to that erratic moment of losing all self-control and she eagerly handed her body completely over to him to have his way with. And oh-la la! What a way he had! It was something like nothing else she had ever experienced! She had been so-called French kissed before, but never like he was doing it. The rumor of Frenchmen being the best lovers in the world was no rumor! He left her breathless, exhausted, and completely satisfied. However, it also gave her a craving for more, and she was in no hurry for him to stop with the massaging.

"Awwww madam," he whispered. "You are mistaken. There is nothing wrong with your love making. Maybe you just need someone like me to wake up your feelings."

"Maybe!" Danika agreed. "I'm sure that has to be it!"

When they were through, he helped her down off of the massage table and then hand in hand, they ran to the hot tub and climbed in. He poured them both a tall goblet of wine, handed her hers, and made a toast to her.

"Here's to a very sexy lady!" His amorous smile made her all warm and fuzzy feeling inside again. But, when she clinked her goblet against his and took a long hard swallow of the wine, she hoped it would take away the feeling of culpability that she was suddenly feeling.

It did! Between the wine, Juan's salacious smiles and the relaxing hot tub, she gave little resistance when he put his arms around her and began giving her tender kisses again. The man had to be a sex God or had indulged in special sexual stimulating herbs, because it wasn't long before they were engaged in full blown, hot water sex, and he had as much stamina as before, if not more.

It was a good thing it was a Friday night, and Danika didn't have to report to any one come Saturday morning, because before the night was over they had romped at least four times, but who was counting? He never seemed to wear down. And when she got ready to leave in the early break of dawn, they neither one had had any sleep. She returned to her apartment with a red chaffed neck, hickies covering her breasts, a swollen vulva, and thighs that were so sore, she could hardly walk, and she kept scolding herself for trying to make up for all the lost time of having sex in just one night!

And why she continued to return to his salon every Friday night at six o'clock for a *special* massage over a three month period was even more incomprehensible. But, if she hadn't arrived one night a little bit early, just to see a much younger woman than herself come out of his studio walking just as bull legged as she did each time with a red chaffed neck, she probably would have continued thinking that she was the only one that he was having such wild sex with and would still be keeping those appointments.

"I'm sorry! But, I think you are blaming the wrong person." Ken scoffed, bringing her back to the present. "*You* were the one that stayed away from home all the time chasing after articles for your dammed magazine. What was I supposed to do?"

"Not go searching for it somewhere else," she retorted.

"Oh! You think I was just supposed to act like I didn't need it?"

"You never complained. How was I supposed to know you were upset with me? I thought you were proud of me for trying to help us get ahead. We were both over loaded with college debt and house payments. And after Jani came along we struggled all the more trying to keep up at the country club and giving her things that we neither one had."

"I guess we both failed. Didn't we?" Ken sighed.

"It all depends on what you think we failed in."

"Keeping in contact with each other while we were married!" he replied.

"Well, it's too late now, so stop complaining about it."

He shook his head. "I'm not complaining! I'm just saying….!" He hesitated. "Maybe I am complaining. I don't know. I guess in the back of my mind I was hoping it wasn't too late for us to maybe think about what happened and try to correct it."

They sat there, just staring at each other for several seconds before she said, "How did you know that I wasn't happy about becoming a Grandma?"

"It was pretty evident. I just hope Jani didn't pick up on it when you were talking to her."

"I tried to be discreet."

"Good!" Then he stood up. "I suppose I had better head back to work. I have a big court case starting tomorrow." He picked up the empty food boxes and threw them in the trash, and then he picked up both plates and placed them in the sink. Danika tried standing up, but the room started whirling around her, so she grabbed the table to steady herself.

"Are you alright?" Ken quickly grabbed her around the waist and held her until she felt like she was stabilized.

"I…I think I'll be okay!"

"That's what you get for drinking so much on an empty stomach," he scolded. "Better let me help you to bed before I leave."

"You just want to try to get inside my PJ's don't you?" She gave him an ardent grin.

"Yes! I want to get inside your PJ's. But not today! I'll take a rain check."

Danika let him help her into her bedroom and on to the bed. And the last thing she remembered was him giving her a quick kiss on the forehead before leaving the room.

CHAPTER FOUR

Danika woke up to the ring tone of her cell phone, and automatically reached for it on the bed side stand. But her fumbling didn't find it, and it took her a couple of seconds to remember how she had gotten to bed, and how she had left it laying on her desk in the den. Upon glancing at the alarm clock on the stand she saw that it was 6:30 AM. Who on earth would be calling her this time of the morning? Jani? Tara? Or was it the nursing home where her mother laid in a bed suffering with the last stage of Alzheimer's disease?

She swung her legs over the edge of the bed and sat up. But that had been a mistake, because instantly, demons were pounding both sides of her head with sledge hammers, reminding her of how much wine she had drank the day before. She quickly lay back down. The phone had quit ringing, so why hurry to answer it? If it was an emergency, whoever it was would call back or leave a voice message.

She had just closed her eyes when the annoying ring started up again. "Damn!" she swore as she slowly rose up this time to set on the edge of the bed. After determining that the pounding was going to remain there, no matter how slowly she moved, she stood up and felt just like she had when she was plagued with that horrible disease called morning sickness through the whole nine months of her pregnancy with Jani. Ugh! Forget the phone! Only one thought arose in her head, and that was to reach the bathroom as quickly as she could.

After getting herself pulled together and her face washed with a warm wet washcloth, she made her way to the den to see who had been calling her so early in the morning. It had a number that she didn't recognize posted on the screen, so she hesitated on calling it back. It had to be the nursing home. Sometimes when they called, the phone would have "unidentified caller" scrolled across it. She inhaled a deep breath to brace herself for the call.

She had placed her mother in one of the top rated nursing homes for Alzheimer's Disease in the Des Moines Area, just a couple of years ago, shortly after Jani's wedding, when her mother had been found by the highway patrol walking along highway #141 with just a nighty and a pair of slippers during an early morning snow storm. It had been by the grace of God that her mother had been found as quickly as she was, or she might have frozen to death or died shortly thereafter from pneumonia.

Danika knew that it was only a matter of time before her mother passed away, as she was losing weight due to the brain shutting down and not passing on the signal to swallow when they fed her. Maybe that was a good thing. The funds that her Dad had left for her mother to live off of was quickly being depleted with the eight grand plus, that it cost each month for her care. Plus, her mother was past recognizing anybody and anything and no longer had any quality of life, and it broke Danika's heart every time she visited, because her mother had always been so active and loved by so many people. But, Danika vowed that once the funds had been used up, she would continue seeing that her mother's care was taken care of out of her own pocket. She refused to place her mother in a less quality care facility just because of money issues.

Her mother had stood beside her throughout all of her marital problems and the whole time she had been trying to get this magazine up and running. Even when Danika just knew that she couldn't survive another day of the turmoil, her mother was always there to coach her on. She had been a strong willed woman that had made it through the eighties when Danika's dad was ill with cancer and yet continued to still struggle bringing in a decent income with his business as a stock broker. Even though her mother lived in Grimes, she was active in helping with fund raisers of all kinds in all of Dallas and Polk Counties. She would give Danika the inside passes to all the charity events for the hospitals, Science Center, Art Center, and political events just to help Danika meet dignitaries and get the scoop for good articles for the magazine. Yes, Danika owed her mother a lot for standing beside her and supporting her efforts.

Danika slowly touched the missed call dot and heard it start ringing, preparing herself for the worse.

"How do you feel? Are you okay?" The deep male voice on the other end took her by surprise.

"How do you think I feel?" she snapped. "And why are you calling me this early?" The sound of his voice even after all these years still made her heart zing around in her chest like a bumble bee, and for some reason, it irritated her and she wasn't sure if she was irritated with him for contacting her again, or herself for still feeling this way about him.

"I just wanted to make sure you were okay before I left for work."

"Why do you suddenly care?"

"You know? That's exactly what I kept asking myself all night, and I haven't the slightest idea of how to answer that. I don't know why I'm concerned about you. I just am. I don't like seeing you like you were yesterday. That just isn't you."

"Well, get over it. I can take care of myself."

"And, that's what the problem is with you. You don't think you need anybody, when in actuality, I think you do."

"Don't you have an important meeting or something that you are missing?"

"Actually, I have a court date early this morning, and then I was wondering if you felt up to meeting me for lunch today."

"No! I don't even feel like going to work today."

"See? That's not like you!"

"You don't know me at all. There are a lot of days I work from my computer here at home instead of going into the office. That's the glory of owning your own business and being able to delegate the work load to others."

"There's an AAA meeting tonight here in Johnston. I'll go with you if you want to get started."

Danika just about flipped! "I told you that I don't need any of those, and the only AAA meetings that I am going to attend are right here."

She could envision him frowning on the other end when he said, "I don't understand."

"Sure you do! At home! Alone! Asleep! That's the only triple A's I'm going to attend to tonight."

She heard him chuckling, and that irritated her even more.

"Okay! I'm sorry for waking you up. I just figured that you were already up and getting ready to leave for work. I'll talk to you later!" With that, his disgustingly cheery voice ended and the phone went dead.

Danika went to the kitchen and placed a tiny plastic pod of dark Columbian coffee in her Keurig coffee maker and pressed the button. But much to her disgust, she had to jump back when she realized that the coffee was spraying all over her and the counter top because she had been so deep in thought that she had neglected to place a coffee cup under the spout. She hurried and grabbed a dish towel and threw it under the steaming brew gushing from the spigot. She was at least smart enough to know that she would get scalded if she dared placing a cup under it now that it was too late. So all she could do was stand back and cuss while the towel soaked up some, but not all, of the scalding brown brew. When it was done running, she carefully picked up the corners of the steaming towel with the tips of her thumb and forefinger and threw it into the sink. Then grabbing a wad of paper towels, she finished wiping the floor and counter top. She would wash her silk pajamas another day, when she had more ambition.

Deciding against making more coffee, Danika went back to the bedroom and called her office. She knew no one would be there, but she left a message for Tara, so she could just go back to bed and forget about the outside world for at least another couple of hours. It was Friday. And it was a known fact that Fridays at work weren't as productive as other days. So she guessed it wouldn't hurt just this once, for the mice to have a day to play while this cat was away. Besides, they had all put in a busy month claiming articles and getting them to her before the deadline.

"You have reached the office of The Complex and Elaborate," Tara's professional sweet voice sounded on the recording. "Our hours are from eight to five, Central Standard Time, Monday through Friday. If you wish to leave a message and have the department extension number that you are trying to reach, please punch in the number at the sound of the tone. Otherwise, you may simply leave a message and a number you can be reached at, and we will return your call just as soon as possible."

"Tara, this is Danika. That head ache I left with yesterday has turned into a good case of the flu. So, I won't be in today. Please tell Josh to send the layout by courier to me today, and I will go over it this weekend. If you have to, just take cash out of the petty drawer to pay the Quizno's delivery in case they don't let you charge, and I will replace it on Monday. Thank you."

Never before had Danika ever called in with the red bottle flu. What had she been thinking? Maybe Ken was right. Maybe she *did* need to go to one of those damned AAA meetings. Or better yet, maybe she needed to see a shrink. Or…., maybe she needed a special massage by her favorite Frenchman. If so, would he still find her attractive enough to suffice? Or would he hold it against her for not returning or calling him after she saw that cute chick come out of his office walking the way she was?

Inhaling a deep breath, she returned to bed, curled up hugging her *State Fair* teddy bear, and dozed back to sleep, hoping when she woke up the next time, she would feel better.

It was almost noon when Danika woke up. She didn't realize she had been so tired. Maybe it was because she had had very little sleep since she had received the package from Jani. Who would believe that being notified that you were about to become a grandmother could be so devastating? She grabbed her father's Double X sized, red plaid, flannel robe out of the closet, and wrapped it around her. It hung big and loose on her, with the waist line hanging down around her buttocks, but it was the only thing she had left to remember him by, except pictures and memories, and she had held on to it when she cleaned out her mother's home before selling it. She didn't have the heart to throw it in the Goodwill Box. Besides, it was faded, so no one would want to buy it anyway. She doubted that the Goodwill store would get more than fifty cents for it. Even old and faded, it was worth much more than that to her.

She hadn't been that old when he passed away, so she didn't have a whole lot of memories to go on. She just remembered that he was always busy and didn't get to spend much time with her. He had always stood tall in her eyes, so she wasn't sure just how tall he really was, but she remembered he was always kind of pudgy and laughed a lot. And if he didn't spend a lot of time with her mother, her mother must not have cared, because she never complained about it and made up for it by being involved in all the community affairs. Now as Danika poured hot water in a cup and stirred her Earl Gray tea bag into it so it could steep, she wondered if she had gotten her work ethics from her dad. Was that the way that corporate people were supposed to spend their time?

Danika jumped when the intercom buzzer sounded. Surely, Josh hadn't gotten the layout sent to her already.

"Yes?"

"Special delivery from Panera here!" a familiar deep voice boomed through the box.

"I didn't know Panera delivered," she stalled. "Besides, I didn't order anything. You must have the wrong address." She didn't want Ken to see her like this.

"Danika! It's Ken. Let me in."

"Oh!" she tried to sound surprised. She didn't want him to know that she was actually excited about seeing him again. "In that case, come on up."

In just the time that it took to ride the elevator to the sixth floor to her apartment, he was outside her door, knocking, and she hadn't had enough time to run a comb through her tangled hair or race to the bedroom to grab a different robe.

He had been equally excited to lay eyes on her again. Even in the state that she had been in yesterday when he left her, once more he felt needed by her, and he had all he could do to refrain from taking advantage of her when he laid her on that king sized bed. It looked much too big for one person, and he was sure that he needed to be in it with her. He had spent the bigger time of the night just reminiscing about the first bed that they had ever owned. They hadn't even cared that they could only afford a full size mattress to lie on the floor the first year of their marriage. It had served its purpose well, and what he wouldn't give to go back to that again with her.

He cringed when she opened the door. Her hair hadn't been combed; her eyes were baggy and bloodshot; yesterday's makeup was distorted; and she was wearing an old pair of terry cloth slippers. Even then, she still looked beautiful to him. But when he took a second glance at the faded man's robe she was wearing, he surmised that she had another man in her life that wore it whenever he visited. Hell, maybe he even lived here with her, and had been gone to work during Ken's visit yesterday.

"Nice robe," he scowled when he brushed past her.

"Thanks," she grinned, assuming he was being his usual self and was making fun of her for the way that she looked. "I put it on just for you."

He ignored her and walked to the kitchen with her trailing behind, and sat a white sack down on the table.

"I thought you said you were going to be in court today?"

"The defense's key witness didn't show up, so the Judge gave him until Monday to find her."

"What's your case about?"

"You know I'm not supposed to divulge that kind of information to you," he frowned as he reached in the sack.

"My magazine doesn't lower itself to printing gossip," she retorted, and took the square Styrofoam container he was handing her.

"Remember about a year ago when that cop was accused of shooting his wife because they were involved in a children's custody battle?"

Danika nodded.

"Well, defense claims that he couldn't have done it, because he was doing undercover work at the time. He claims that it had to be her boyfriend that shot her, because she had just dumped him."

"So, can't the police department verify that?"

"They are hesitant, because they say his life will be in danger if it comes out where he was working at."

"Still?"

"I know! It's been a doozy of a case to try to prove, or disprove, as far as that goes."

"So, who's his witness?"

"She's a call girl at one of the bars down town that we've been trying to close down."

"Ahhhhh! She's afraid of being sent to jail for prostitution if she appears in court isn't she?"

"Not only that, but I guess she's afraid the bar owner will fire her as a waitress if she testifies, and says she needs the job. I'm not so sure she's not afraid for her own life. Anyway, I thought a grilled chicken dinner salad might taste good to you!"

"Do you want some hot tea with me? Or, I have iced tea, coffee or wine that you can have."

"Iced tea will do," he smiled, just as the entrance buzzer sounded again. His heart sank. Was this the other man in her life?

CHAPTER FIVE

Danika opened the door to an unsuspecting delivery boy. He took one look at her and thrust the plastic clipboard to her at arm's length.

"I need a signature in that window!" he said as he pointed to the dotted line. He then handed her a rubber stylus and watched her sign before quickly turning on one heel and hurrying away, rubbing his free hand on his pants as if hoping to wipe any germs away. He left the large manila package just lying on the floor in front of the door.

Hmmmm! She should probably have a talk with Josh about the courier service they were using.

When Danika returned to the kitchen she couldn't quite figure out what was going through Ken's head as he stood leaning against the counter with arms folded across his chest.

"Is something wrong?"

"I didn't know if I should try hiding in the closet, or just what?"

"Why on earth would you want to hide in the closet?" she frowned.

"I thought it might be the man that belongs to that robe you are wearing, and I can tell by the size of it that he is bigger than me!" A look of relief crossed his face as he took his suit jacket off, hung it on the back of his chair, and loosened his tie.

Danika laughed out loud.

"What's so funny?" he frowned.

Did she tell him or keep him wondering? She decided to tell him since she was starting to enjoy having his unexpected visits, even though it was against her better judgment.

"Is this the way you felt when you were having your extra-marital affair with Sonya?"

"Okay! Not funny! So what are you *really* laughing at?"

"This not-so-glamorous robe belonged to my dad. I brought it home with me when I sold all of my mother's belongings."

A large grin creased his face. "Whew! That makes me feel better all the way around."

What he meant by that, she wasn't sure, but she decided against asking. She pulled a tall glass out of the cupboard, placed it under the ice spigot on the freezer, and then rummaged in the fridge for the pitcher of tea that she had made a couple of days before. She filled the glass with tea and then remembering that it was Ken that she was pouring it for, put a spoonful of artificial sweetener in it and stirred before handing it to him. Then she picked up her own cup of now tepid Earl Gray tea, and sat down across the small table from him.

"How did you know that I liked Panera's salads?" she asked as she picked at the grilled chicken salad that Ken had brought for her.

"Everyone likes Panera Bread's soups and salads," he grinned, "so I took a chance on it."

Danika wasn't sure about the way that it was settling in her stomach, so she just minced and picked at it, only eating part of it.

"At this rate, I'm going to owe you a meal. You've fed me now two days in a row," she stated in a peevish tone.

"And I want a steak at the Texas Road House," he teased, refusing to acknowledge the way she had said it.

After she found out that he wasn't going to let her bad mood influence him in any way, their conversation relaxed and they started talking as if nothing had ever come between them. She told him some of the stories that her journalists were covering, and he told her a little more about the case of the undercover cop and what some of the problems were in proving anything. He personally still felt that the cop was guilty because he couldn't account well enough for his whereabouts at the time of the murder, plus his stories seemed to keep conflicting. But at the same time, his office couldn't come up with enough evidence to have a clear cut case. There were too many circumstances casting doubts, which meant that there were enough to keep a jury from finding a verdict of guilty like Ken wanted.

When he had finished with his salad and iced tea, Ken stood up and started clearing the table. Danika had long been done with hers, since her stomach could only handle about a third of it.

"Do you feel up to getting out of town for a while?" he asked.

"What are you calling out of town, and how long is awhile?"

"Since I don't have anything special going on this afternoon, and since you aren't off searching for a story of some kind, I thought maybe we could take a drive out to Saylorville Lake and see what all is going on. You used to enjoy watching the water go over the spillway." He replied.

"I can't! I have this layout to go over so that it's ready to go to print on Monday. I'm sorry," she apologized. Not only did she have the manuscript to sort out, but she wasn't sure her head and stomach could handle the noise and vibration of standing next to the surging water as it went over the dam.

"Nothing new," he shook his head. "I should be used to it by now."

"Well maybe just for a couple of hours, it won't hurt," she said when she saw the disappointment on his face.

"Are you serious?"

"You better take me up on it before I change my mind," she teased. "You've caught me at one of my weaker moments."

"You can even go in your father's robe if you want. Let's go!" he grinned.

"I would like to, but I'll pass," Danika grinned. And then she added, "Make yourself at home," as she hurried toward her bedroom to grab a quick shower and change into something that was cool for this hot summer day.

Who was she trying to fool? She was just as excited to be going with him, as the gleam in his eyes showed he was to be taking her, so she not only wanted something cool, but she wanted to put on something sexy. After all, as soon as she was labeled Grandma, she probably wouldn't dare wear anything that made her look attractive and irresistible. And right now, she couldn't remember how her mother used to dress after Jani came along.

Thirty minutes later when she walked into the living room dressed in a white satin tank top, a pair of pressed navy blue cotton shorts, and a pair of white sequined flip flops, Ken whistled in admiration, and she could feel the heat rise up her neck and into her cheeks. She had hurriedly spread foundation over her face to cover any flaws that might be trying to appear, and applied eye liner and mascara. No eye shadow today and no blush. Now she didn't need it. Instead of taking the time to dry her hair and using the curling iron on it, she pulled it back and wound a pony tail tie around it at the nap of her neck. No girlish pony tail either. She had sorted through several drawers to even find the shorts. She lived in business suits, spandex gym clothes, or white denim capris and white cotton tanks to play golf. She only wore fancy dresses when there was something formal to attend. But shorts? Her life no longer called for shorts and flip flops so they were buried in the very bottom of one of the dresser drawers. After all, when you are competing in a man's world, you have to look professional at all times, no matter what the cost or convenience.

She was surprised when she entered Ken's house. The atmosphere pretty much looked the same as when she had lived in it and decorated it. The living room furniture was newer and different, but the drapes, pictures, and carpeting were the same. She meandered into the kitchen while Ken went to change his clothes. The breakfast set was still the solid oak wood with the same chairs, and the décor of her red apples theme that she had enjoyed when they were first married, was still prominent. Evidently Sonya hadn't cared enough to change things to her way of thinking, or else Ken didn't let her. Either way, Danika knew that had it been her, she would have changed things completely so that the house had her and Ken's personalities, instead of his former wife's.

From the kitchen, she peeked into the den where the fireplace was and seen the complete office still as it had been when she was there. On the mantle of the fireplace there were several pictures of Jani. Jani in each year's basketball uniform, holding the ball; and in her softball uniforms with the entire team that started out together when they were in sixth grade, and stayed together as a team all through high school. They had even made it to the state tournaments and gotten beaten out by two points in their senior year. Danika had been able to take off long enough that day to watch them play and see the disappointment and tears when the game was over. She herself had to wipe away tears as she could only imagine how the girls had felt. In fact, her throat had been so constricted when the game was over that she had went straight to her car and avoided trying to push through the crowd to give Jani a hug, only to be accused later by Ken of not showing up or making an appearance.

Also on the mantle was Jani's high school graduation picture, a picture of her and Rick when they had repeated the same vows that Danika and Ken had twenty two years earlier, and Jani in her cap and gown when she graduated from college. But, what shocked Danika more than anything was the five by eight picture of her, Ken, and Jani that had been taken when Jani had turned one year old. It was the first family picture that they had taken together and it seemed to be the perfect indication of pure happiness for years to come. So, what happened?

Danika picked Jani's college graduation picture up and was admiring how pretty her brown haired, blue eyed, daughter was. Not only was she pretty, but was the perfect specimen of what a good daughter was supposed to be like. Every parent worries about their children getting involved in drugs and alcohol as they grow up. And just about every parent tries to do the best they know how to raise them to be responsible adults. Jani had passed the test on all aspects.

"At least we did one thing right during our marriage, didn't we?" Ken smiled as he walked up behind her, looking breath takingly handsome in his White Henley knit shirt and blue denim shorts. "We produced a wonderful daughter that is just full of love, and now she's going to share that love with us by giving us another little girl to hold and cherish. And who knows, maybe even a boy or two before they are done. Wouldn't that be great?"

Danika knew that Ken had always wanted to have another baby, in hopes that it would be a boy. But she had never consented, because having another baby just couldn't fit into the schedule that she was keeping. Maybe if she would have consented and worked it in somehow, they would still be married. But after the divorce, she had consoled herself by thinking it was better that they didn't have but only one child to go through what Jani did.

"I suppose. Maybe someday you'll get that boy that you always wanted," she answered.

"Maybe," his voice sounded hopeful. He picked up Jani's picture again and said, "She *is* a beautiful girl, isn't she? Just like her mother!"

"She doesn't look anything like me," Danika shook her head. "She's much prettier and looks like you."

"Oh!" a mischievous grin creased his face. "I knew she got her good looks from someone. I just didn't know I could take credit for it!"

Danika smacked his bare arm. "You know darned well she's your daughter."

"Yes," he gave her a tender smile. "I never doubted for a second that she was my daughter."

Danika scowled. "How could you have possibly thought otherwise?"

"You were gone so much. There were plenty of times that I sat here wondering who you were seeing?"

"Are you telling me that you actually thought I was cheating on you?"

"Well..." His face turned red. "Not necessarily before she was born. But after that, I did."

"Oh, Ken! You silly man! Not once did I ever want or even think about seeing anyone else. You were the love of my life and I always came home to you."

"Ouch! I really screwed up, didn't I?" Then he slipped his hands around her waist and said, "I wish there was some way that I could make things up to you."

"We're both wearing big people's pants now, so no sense in traipsing backwards. We can only go forward."

"You're right," he whispered. Then he bent down and gave her a light tender kiss. When she didn't reject or back away, he gave her another, longer, tasty one. And then another, and another, with each one pressing firmer, searching for answers. And then he slipped his arms completely around her, pulling her body in tighter against his, with kisses becoming hungrier. His eyes were hooded and his breathing erratic and she knew what he was hungry for. And the problem was she was hungry for it too!

They never made it to Saylorville Lake.

Morning passed and finally by ten o'clock, they were stepping into the shower to recoup from the night's tussling.

"Well, now you know that I don't need Viagra, and Grandmas and Grandpas can still enjoy sex!" Ken grinned as they stepped in under the pulsating water together. "And you survived the night without a drop of Yellow Tail! How's that for coincidence?"

"Whatever you want to call it, it's better than attending any AAA meetings, "Danika grinned.

"We did miss the meeting last night, didn't we? And you didn't get to attend your own personal AAA meeting," Ken chuckled. "And I can't say that I'm unhappy about it."

Danika didn't answer. She just pursed her lips and started lathering herself up with his fragrant Old Spice soap designed just for men. It wasn't going to make her smell quite like she would like, but at least it would remove the sweaty BO that both of them had incurred from all the extra exercising that they had participated in during the night. Ken's eyes followed what she was doing for several minutes before he took the soap away from her and started doing his own massaging of her body with it. And when he was done, he handed her the soap so she could do the same to him---just like old times, so many years ago. And just like old times, it led to another splashing, love making, romp in the tub.

Danika didn't care that she was letting her Saturday get away from her and she still hadn't looked at the layout of all the articles so they could go to print first thing Monday morning. She had forgotten all about the queasy stomach from the red bottle flu, and she no longer had the headache. *Hmmmm!*

"Do you still like Egg McMuffins?" Ken asked when then finally emerged from the tub.

"I haven't had one for years," Danika admitted, as she hurriedly wrapped a bath sheet around her body and then wrapped another around her hair turban style to absorb the water. "Why?"

"I thought maybe we could go through the drive up window at McDonalds on our way out to Saylorville and then look for a picnic table in the shade where we could eat. Would you like that?"

"Sounds good to me," Danika grinned. It was something that they had done a lot while they were dating and trying to survive on a college kid's allowance. Only back then, sometimes it ended up with a long hike and a romp in the tall grass away from any other human beings. She could suddenly feel her age creeping up on her. She didn't think she could stand a long hike or another romp in the grass today. Even though she was used to working out in the gym, her thighs were feeling the after effects of the long eventful night.

In fact, a horrible thought crossed through her mind. They hadn't used any type of protection like they had in their earlier days when they were tussling so much. She had read once that a man with a normal testosterone level, at any age, had a ninety five percent chance of producing strong healthy sperm. So did this mean that after last night and this morning, she had a three hundred percent chance of being pregnant? Heaven forbid! Why hadn't she been thinking? Now was *not* the time to be worrying about it! She should have been worrying about it *before* she stripped her clothes off and so willingly climbed into his bed. Just the thought of it made her feel sick to her stomach all over again.

"Are you okay?" Ken asked when the color of her face suddenly turned ashen.

"I just need a cup of strong coffee," she replied, trying to avoid eye contact with him. Then she added, "Actually, what I need is a tall glass of Yellow Tail, or Gray Goose over ice with Bloody Mary mix, or maybe a tequila sunrise!"

"No you don't!" a deep frown furrowed across his face. "What you need is to go to recovery!"

"Recovery from what? You?"

"No!" His frown deepened. "Yourself! You need to get your life straightened out!"

"Nothing's wrong with my life, thank you very much!"

"Anybody that needs a drink of alcohol the first thing in the morning needs to go to recovery, and I'm going to see to it that you do!"

Now Danika was frowning as hard as Ken, and the rebellious side of her that she had always possessed kicked in, over riding her better judgment. "And just how do you think you are going to see to that?"

"By staying with you for the next two weeks while you start through it."

"Excuse Me? But I thought I just heard you say you were going to stay with me for the next two weeks!"

"You heard me right! I didn't stutter!"

"And just how do you plan on doing that? You have a large court case coming up and I have a company to run!"

"Your company can go to Hell if it can't survive without you long enough to get yourself straightened out; and I can get one of the assistant DAs to take my case. I can follow the case through Skype right from your living room."

"Okay! Okay!" she threw up her hands. "Let's just step back and look at this again. First, get it through your thick skull that I am *not* an alcoholic, and I do *not* need recovery time. I only said I needed a drink because of what was passing through my head. I *don't* want to be a grandmother yet, and I absolutely *don't* want to have another baby. But the odds of that after last night are over three hundred percent. So right at the moment, yes, I would like to drown my life with alcohol until I can grasp it all."

The look on his face plainly told that he didn't believe her on the not being an alcoholic part. And at the same time, it was as if he had suddenly been slapped in the face, realizing that he might be a new daddy again. Only, just like being a grandfather, he would probably be thoroughly pleased with the situation. But then again, she wasn't sure. He wasn't acting overly joyed about it like she thought he might.

CHAPTER SIX

"That settles it!" a big scowl creased Ken's face. "You are definitely going to get help. Pregnant mothers can't drink alcohol."

"I didn't say I was pregnant!" Danika snapped. "I said after last night, there could be a three hundred percent chance that I am."

"Well until you know for sure, I'm going to stay with you to make sure that you don't indulge. We aren't taking any chances!"

"Ken…!"

"Don't argue! You know as well as I do that this is the best thing that could happen to us."

Danika frowned. *The best thing? She was too young to be a grandmother, and too old to be the mother of a new baby! How ironic was that? And to make things even worse, Ken was insisting that she was an alcoholic just because she had over indulged yesterday when he happened to drop by. Plus, if he thought he is going to move in with her to try controlling her as if nothing had ever happened between them, he had another think coming! What else could go wrong? More so, what was she going to do about it?*

"I refuse to argue with you on an empty stomach," Danika finally replied as she traipsed to the side of the bed where her clothes were still laying on the floor.

About that time Ken's phone rang and he excused himself to leave the room to take it. When he returned, he said, "Nothing serious, my private investigator just had some information for my case coming up Monday that he thought I should know about right away."

Danika just kind of nodded her head and thought nothing more about it. She was still thinking about the conversation they were having before he took the call.

"So how does breakfast at Perkin's instead of McDonald's sound?" Ken asked.

"Where ever we go or whatever we do, I'm not going to argue about being an alcoholic, and you *aren't* going to move in with me!"

"You either go kicking or screaming to recovery somewhere or you move in with me! It's your choice!" Ken retorted. "I don't want my granddaughter to know that her grandma is an alcoholic."

By now, Danika was beginning to see red! "I'll settle for breakfast at Perkins, I'm buying, I'm not an alkie, and I'm neither moving in with you or you with me!"

"No! You don't get out of it that easy," Ken wasn't smiling. "Buying my breakfast won't get you anywhere."

Danika heaved a big sigh, and finished getting dressed, refusing to bend to his wishes by giving him the satisfaction of an answer. She let her damp hair just fall loose on her shoulders and down her back, slipped into her flip flops, and left the bedroom without worrying about wearing any makeup, since she didn't have any with her to worry about. The problem right now was that she was at his discretion since she had rode in his car to his house and decided to spend the night with him instead of going home like a good girl should have done.

"As soon as we eat, I need to get home to get started on the layout of our next edition," she called over her shoulder as she left the bedroom.

"I'll help you!" he called back.

Danika stopped short and turned around. "Are you serious?" she started laughing. "I could have sworn that you said you would help me!"

"What's so funny about that?" Ken frowned as he joined her in the hallway. "I can determine what looks good and what doesn't. Just show me how you do it and I can help you."

Once more, Danika didn't give him the satisfaction of an answer. She just smirked and headed for the front door.

Ken drove them to the nearest Perkins restaurant on Merle Hay Road. It had been years since Danika had been in that restaurant, and a lot had changed. She remembered when it was all booths and there was a miniature jukebox at every table that they could play. They had patronized it a lot when she was married to him, but since she had moved to one of the inner city apartment buildings, she hadn't had any reason to be in this part of town these days.

Shortly after being seated by a hostess and receiving their first cup of coffee to get them started, Danika noticed a stoutly man, probably in his early to middle thirties, come in and sit in a booth not too far from them across the aisle. She guessed him to be a biker, since he had long dark brown hair that hung in a ponytail down his back, his face was covered with a heavy matching beard, wore earrings in both ears, had a red bandana tied around his head, wore faded blue jeans, and wore a black leather jacket with silver epaulettes across the shoulders and on the pockets. It didn't strike her as odd since the restaurant was only about a half mile or so from the two interstates that crisscrossed across the north side of the city. A lot of travelers patronized this restaurant because it was so convenient.

But, it seemed that every time she looked his direction he was watching her, and it gave her the heebie-jeebies. She tried to ignore him at the same time she tried consoling herself that she was just being paranoid because she was tired due to lack of sleep for the last couple of nights.

Finally when she had finished her meal and drank her third cup of coffee, she excused herself to go to the women's restroom. Ken followed behind her to pay for the meal at the same time, since one had to walk past the cash register to get to the restrooms.

When Danika returned to the front of the restaurant, the man in the leather jacket was at the cash register paying for his meal, and she had to walk behind him to get out the door where Ken stood waiting for her. Why it was bothering her, she had no idea, because usually she never gave people around her a second thought. She was always intermingled with the public and people of all makes and models one way or another, and if anything, she enjoyed watching them. It was her way of knowing what was happening around her. There was always a story there somewhere just waiting to be written.

Danika heaved a big sigh and scolded herself for feeling the way she was and walked past the man. But just as she did so, he swung around so fast and hard that he knocked her sprawling into a large fig tree that was standing in a huge planter by the entry door.

"Oh, Ma'am!" he grabbed her arm and tugged on her to help her up. "I'm so sorry! I didn't realize you were behind me!" he exclaimed. His voice was deep and sincere, and Danika had trouble understanding if he was serious or if he had done it on purpose. He helped her stand up and apologized again, and then picked up her tote bag and handed it to her as Ken came charging back through the door to see what had happened, demanding an answer from the stranger.

"This is between the lady and me," the man in leather scowled. "So butt out of it."

Telling Ken to *butt out of it* was the wrong thing for the stranger to do, because Ken wasn't in the habit of *butting out* of people's business when it came to something he felt was criminal mischief.

"It's okay, Ken!" Danika quickly spit out, when she saw the fire in Ken's eyes begin to create a confrontation between the two men. "I'm not hurt. Maybe a little shaken, but not hurt!"

"Well, next time try to be more careful before you carelessly go swinging around in public!" Ken glared at the stranger.

Once more the stranger nodded at Danika and said, "I'm really sorry ma'am. Enjoy your day." With that, he hurried out the door and into the parking lot.

"What a jerk!" Ken frowned as he took ahold of Danika's hand and led her out to his car. "Someone needs to teach him a lesson!"

"I don't think he did it on purpose," Danika soothed. "I should have waited for him to leave or else not walked so close to him. After all, he had his back turned toward me. He didn't know I was there."

"I suppose you are right," Ken smiled.

"I know I'm right!" Danika replied. "So now forget about him and get me home so I can get busy."

"But we haven't been to Saylorville yet!" Ken argued.

"And whose fault is that?" Danika teased as she climbed into the car.

Ken grinned and then leaned over and gave her another quick kiss on the cheek before settling into his seat and hooking his seat belt. "Okay! I'm guilty, and I am not even sorry one little iota about it."

Danika had been right. As she and Ken settled into his car, the stranger was leaving the parking lot on a shiny black, trimmed in silver, Harley Davidson Motorcycle and headed north toward the interstate.

The ride to her apartment was quiet, and Danika knew Ken was still thinking about the stranger in the restaurant. He followed her into her apartment and waited for her to spread the papers held by the manila folder out on the huge cherry wood dining room table before he said anything.

"Okay!" Danika sighed. "Here is the beginning of the manuscript." She pointed to page number one. "My job now is to see to it that it all flows along for easy reading and that the continuances are placed where they say they're supposed to be."

Ken nodded and slowly meandered behind her as she skimmed over the layout. Out of the corner of her eye she saw him reach down and retrieve a sheet of the manuscript off the table and began reading it.

"Don't be moving anything!" she scolded. "It's too easy to forget where it goes."

"Who is Marty Vineteri?" Ken asked, ignoring her.

"He is one of the newer free-lance writers that enter articles every so often when he gets a chance. He also writes for the Des Moines Register once in a while," Danika answered. "Why?"

"I thought you said you didn't print gossip!"

"We don't!"

"Do you read everything that comes in to be printed?"

"Usually! I make the final decision as to what goes into production. That's what we are doing now."

"And you allowed this article?"

Danika grabbed the sheet from his hand. She didn't want him to know that this was probably one of the very few times that she hadn't read what was going into the magazine. She had been so upset about Jani's baby, that she had just handed it on to the production team to get it printed. She quickly skimmed over the page.

"What's wrong with it?" she frowned.

Ken jerked it back out of her hand. "It's an article that can get you and your Mr. Vineteri in trouble or even killed!"

"What?" Danika jerked the sheet back. "How?"

"It's about Emanuel Vasquez, the suspected drug cartel Lord that's trying to muscle his way into Iowa. It's not something that goes into your type of magazine, and I don't think it's something that is supposed to be in print. Not even in a daily newspaper like the Register. Vineteri has some things written in here that don't make sense. You can't print this."

Danika skimmed over the page and the picture of an iron gate with a gravel road leading into a timbered property. Also, the page showed a beautiful estate at the end of the road with a large circle driveway. Danika estimated the estate to be worth several million dollars.

"What's wrong with this?" she asked. "This is the kind of pictures and articles that we write about all the time."

"Maybe nothing is wrong with the pictures, but the article reveals where the mansion is, and everyone knows that any drug lord doesn't want anyone to know where he resides. In fact, this article even shows how many body guards there are that protect the property. Look closer at the balcony of the house."

"We have the right to write and print anything. It's called freedom of speech. Remember? Besides, I'm sure that Mr. Vineteri got permission from the owner before he took the pictures."

"Dani! You don't understand! I don't care that the estate is exposed. It's your life I'm concerned about if Vasquez gets ahold of this."

"There's no way he can get ahold of it before it goes to print." Danika continued to argue. "Besides, I know that if I jerk it out of my magazine, Marty will take it to the newspaper. Why can't my magazine get the credit?"

Ken sadly shook his head. "Okay," he conceded. "Print the damned thing. I just hope you know what you are doing."

"You just worry too much!" Danika smiled, knowing she had won the argument.

"It's my business to worry. You may know all about elaborate million dollar homes and billionaire businesses, but you don't know criminals like I do. And believe me when I say your life may be in jeopardy if it goes to print."

Danika re-read the article one more time. "All this article exposes is a business man's estate and tells a little bit about his business. He's a guru in technology and has several employees that work for him putting together a couple of new games for the play station that is coming out on the market before Christmas. How can that be a crime?"

"That isn't. It's the business that he does behind closed doors that has me concerned!"

"Well, this article is going to print because there is nothing here that incriminates him or me!"

"Okay! Don't say I didn't warn you!" Ken scolded.

CHAPTER SEVEN

Danika did her usual routine of placing a cup under the Keurig coffee maker spout, sticking a cartridge in it and pushing the brew button, sticking a bagel in the toaster to get hot, and pulling the strawberry flavored cream cheese spread, plus a yogurt, from the refrigerator. While the coffee brewed and the bagel toasted, she stepped to the apartment door and stuck her head out in the hall to retrieve the morning newspaper. But this morning, for some reason, she looked both directions down the hallway to be sure all was clear before reaching down to pick the newspaper up off the floor. *Darn Ken! Now he had her worrying about every little thing! Something she had just never done before.*

She had finally convinced Ken that she would be safe, she wasn't going to indulge in any type of alcohol, and since she had to be to work early due to getting the manuscript into print, that there was no reason for him to stay another night. Not only that, but she wasn't sure she could stand another night of having him stay with her. She swore he was still just as obsessed with having sex with her as he had been when they were on their honeymoon. She was used to jogging, golfing, working out at the gym, and playing tennis, but none of those activities made her thighs as sore as they were after spending two nights in bed with him.

It had taken her several years to get over having feelings for him after the divorce. The hurt had cut too deep to fully mend and even to this very day, just hearing his name or having a fleeting memory traipse through her mind would upset her. Now here he was, wanting back into her life again and she was still too much in love with him to say no to all of his wishes. Just like old times. In fact, she had caught herself checking her phone a couple of times, just wishing that he would call to say good morning, even though she had told him that she had a real busy schedule, so she couldn't have lunch with him any time during the week. In the back of her mind she was setting boundaries again for herself, knowing that things would be better all the way around if they didn't get involved again. She couldn't handle a fall again if things didn't work out.

Danika skimmed over the newspaper as she ate her bagel and yogurt. She took the time to brew another cup of coffee so she could search deeper into the newspaper just to see if there was anything in it about another drug lord trying to muscle his way into the Des Moines area. Even though there were no speculations given, there had been a couple more killings over the weekend, and the police were asking for witnesses to come forward. As of yet, they didn't feel that it was gang related. But, Danika knew the area of town that they had taken place in, and in the back of her mind she wondered if it *was* related since there had been more than one incident in that neighborhood the past month. Businesses were being targeted and Danika knew that a couple of them were Mafia owned. Details were being kept hush-hush to the media. Could it be that Marty Vineteri *had* stumbled on to something that the police didn't want the public to know about yet?

As Danika took the elevator to the bottom floor where her car was parked in the garage, she couldn't help but feel that uneasy feeling again that Ken had now instilled into her mind. All was clear as she stepped out of the elevator where several other apartment dwellers were hurrying to their cars, so she felt safe.

Once she was pulling into the parking ramp up the street from her office, she made sure that there were no questionable characters standing around or close to where she was going to park her car, and then made sure it was locked when she finally climbed out and hurried to the elevator to take to her floor level. She had never found herself fearful before, even when she would stay late trying to tie up loose ends in her office. Now here she was this morning, filled with all kinds of fear, just because of some magazine article that had been innocently written by a freelance contributor. Maybe she should stop using freelance writers and just stick to her own employees. But then, freelance writers seemed to bring something to the table that her regular employees couldn't do.

"Are you feeling better?" Tara asked as Danika entered the office.

"Better?"

"Yes! You had the flu. Remember?"

"Yes! Thank you." Danika smiled as she reached for the mail in her basket. "Is there anything I should know about?"

"Well," Tara smiled. "You owe the petty cash drawer money since the Quizno's manager wouldn't let me charge for all the subs on Friday, and you have a man sitting in your office again."

"Is it Ken?" Danika's heart skipped a beat at the thought of seeing him again this morning.

"No," Tara frowned.

"No?"

Tara shook her head. "He says his name is Special Agent Carson." Then she whispered, "I think he is from the FBI."

Now Danika started frowning. What could a special agent from the FBI want with her?

Tara shrugged her shoulders when she saw the questioning look on Danika's face. So heaving a deep sigh to set her mind straight, Danika walked into her office.

A fairly good looking man that stood about five feet ten inches or such stood watching out her window. Danika couldn't help but think how his dark blue eyes looked tired when he turned around to face her, and the lines in his face told her that he was at least forty five years old or maybe older. Whatever his age, something seemed to be taking its toll on him.

"Mr. Carson?" Danika extended her hand. "I'm Danika Bronson. My assistant tells me that you wanted to see me?"

"Yes!" His eyes lit up when he took ahold of her hand and shook it. He seemed surprised as his eyes quickly combed over her. "I'm sorry," he apologized with a sheepish grin on his face. "I guess I was expecting an older woman to enter the room and not one that is…, is…, as young as you."

Danika smiled and passed it off by asking him if he wanted to sit down.

"I just have a few questions to ask you," he returned the smile, "and then I'll be on my way."

So feeling uncomfortable standing in front of him, Danika nodded, so he could continue.

He reached inside his suit jacket and pulled out a picture. "Do you know this man?" he asked.

Danika blinked with surprise. "No. I don't think I've ever had the pleasure."

A deep frown furrowed across Agent Carson's face. "They tell me that he works for you. Is that right?"

"No! I know all of my employees and he isn't one of them." But in the back of her head she knew she had seen him somewhere. And then it hit her! It was the biker at the Perkin's restaurant that had kept watching her and knocked her so ungraciously into the fig tree. She took the picture from him to study it better.

"No! He isn't one of my employees!" she repeated. "Whoever told you that told you wrong!"

"Really?" Agent Carson's tone clearly told her that he didn't believe her. "His name is Andrew Sanchez. But he is also known as Marty Vineteri, and he has been known to write articles for your magazine. Now shall we start over again and this time, don't lie to me."

Danika was shocked. "That's Marty Vineteri? Honestly, I've never met him. He is a free-lance writer that sends us articles to be printed every so often just like he does for other magazines and the daily newspaper."

"And you expect me to believe that you don't know him?"

"Correct. Depending on the size of the article, we just pay him for what he submits to us."

"And how is that?"

"Just like we do all of the free-lance writers that submit articles to us. They send us an article by emailing it to our publication team. If the article is accepted, we send them a check for what we think it is worth. We never meet them face to face. Why are you asking?"

"Never mind," his smile was contagious, and Danika found herself wanting to like him at the same time the red flag went up warning her to stay clear. "So, are you related to Kenneth Bronson, our district attorney?" he changed the subject.

"No! Not anymore." Danika replied. "I'm his ex-wife. Why?"

"Good!" he grinned.

"Good?" Danika frowned.

"I mean..., never mind what I meant," he sobered up. "Thank you for your time, Ms. Bronson. It was nice meeting you." With that he hurried out of the room leaving Danika wondering what was going through the man's mind.

It was then that Danika realized that she still had the manila envelope with the new manuscript tucked under her arm. She walked back out to Tara's desk and handed it to her.

"Would you please see to it that Josh gets this?" Then Danika said, "Also please call Keven and Amanda and tell them to meet me in my office in about twenty minutes."

"Yes Ma'am," Tara responded. Then she said, "What did you say to that man? He shot out of here like the devil was chasing him."

Danika just grinned. "I guess he got all the information that he needed." Then as an afterthought she said, "I need Marty Vineteri's phone number. Can you please look it up and give it to me?"

"Yes Ma'am," Tara answered as Danika walked back into her office.

Danika glanced at her watch and then at her cell phone again. Why she was wishing it would ring with Ken's voice on the other end of the air waves was beyond her comprehension.

Twenty minutes later Keven and Amanda from the publications department were walking into Danika's office. Danika could tell that Amanda was nervous about being called in to see the boss. Usually one didn't get called into Danika's office unless they were about to be fired or if a promotion was due.

"Which one of you okayed the article sent to us by Marty Vineteri?" Danika asked.

"I did," Keven answered. "Is there a problem?"

"I hope not," Danika answered. "I went ahead and authorized his article this time because time was too short to find something to fill in with. But from now on, I want to see anything that comes in from him before it goes any farther. Do you understand?"

Both Keven and Amanda nodded their heads and then Danika excused them to go back to work. She could tell by the look on their faces that they didn't understand why she had just called them on the carpet, but Danika decided it may be better for everyone involved if they didn't know anything about what Ken had told her.

"Danika," it was Tara's voice on the office intercom. "I don't have a house number for Mr. Vineteri. All I have is a cell phone number. Do you want that?"

"Yes!" Danika wrote it on a pad as Tara recited it to her. But when she tried calling it, it instantly went into voice mail instead of him answering.

"Marty, this is Danika Bronson calling. We have never met, but I am the chief editor for the magazine company called The Complex and Elaborate, that you have submitted several articles to. I need to talk to you about the last article that you submitted to us, before it goes to print. Could you please return my call as soon as possible? Thank you." And then Danika gave him both her office number and her cell phone number so that he could call her at any time of the day.

Which never came!

CHAPTER EIGHT

"Ms. Bronson!"

Danika froze right where she stood beside her Red Dodge Viper. She had heard that male voice before, but remembering just where escaped her memory right at the moment. She had left her office right at five o'clock, so that she could be in the parking garage at a busy time, and had looked all directions around the garage when she stepped off the elevator of the third floor level to be sure she was safe from anyone looking suspicious. Now she had just unlocked the car door by remote and was reaching for the handle when he spoke, and it frightened her like she had never been frightened before.

Agent Carson stepped away from the cement pillar in front of Danika's car. "You drive a pretty fancy car, so you need to be more cautious where you park it," he smiled as he took the keys out of her trembling hand. "That could have been anyone hiding behind that pillar!"

"What do you want?" Danika frowned.

"I thought I would buy you a cup of coffee," he replied.

"Now?"

"Yes. Is that a problem?"

"Yes," she answered. "I'm meeting some friends at the Y."

"Well," he pursed his lips. "You'll just have to meet them some other time."

"Who do you think you are?" Danika retorted.

"Someone that's trying to keep you out of trouble," he grinned.

"I'm not in trouble!" Danika snapped. "Besides, I don't really know who you are. And how did you know which car was mine? Have you been stalking me?"

Agent Carson pulled his suit jacket back exposing the badge clipped to his belt again, and then he reached inside the jacket and pulled out a small leather folder that he handed to her. It revealed his picture and credentials. She had guessed right. He was forty six years old, his name was Robert Beau Carson, and was a special agent for the FBI.

"Satisfied?" he asked.

"Okay! You work for the FBI. But that doesn't explain why you are stalking me, and what you want with me."

"The coffee shop is right around the corner." He relocked her car and handed her back the keys. "We can talk while we walk."

"I need to call my friends," Danika objected. "They'll be wondering where I am."

She reached for the phone in her Italian leather handbag, and called Alma and lied, telling her that she had to work late. After convincing Alma that she couldn't make it to work out at the Y with the girls, Danika heaved a deep sigh and said, "Okay. Let's go have coffee." *If she was going to be forced to do something she didn't want to do, she might as well get it over with just as quickly as possible. However, the thought of walking another block or so wasn't really what she wanted to do either.*

"I thought you said Marty Vineteri didn't work for you!" Agent Carson said as they started walking toward the elevator.

"He doesn't!"

"Then why did you call him just as soon as I walked out of your office this morning?"

"Not only are you stalking me, but you better have a damned good reason for tapping into my office phone!" Danika came to a dead stop and glared at him.

"I'm not tapped into your phone! Not yet, anyway," he scowled.

"You better not at all!" Danika warned.

"Why? Are you trying to hide something?"

"Am I under interrogation?"

"No! I just have a few more questions to be answered, plus I just wanted to buy you a cup of coffee. There's nothing wrong with that, is there?"

"It all depends on how much more drilling you are going to do!"

Agent Carson took ahold of Danika's arm and tried directing her to the elevator, but Danika refused to budge.

"Okay," he frowned. "Your Mr. Vineteri is under investigation for trafficking drugs. I just wondered how much you know about it!"

"Nothing!"

"Well, you certainly look guilty of something when you don't want to cooperate and by calling him like you did this morning."

Danika glanced all around the garage, and then said, "Okay! He has an article coming out in my magazine this month that shows pictures of a possible drug lord's estate. Ken saw it and told me not to print it because it reveals too much. But I sent it to publication anyway," she confessed. "I tried to call Marty to warn him about any repercussions the magazine might have, and also that he needed to be careful. But he didn't answer his cell phone."

Agent Carson studied her for a second, and then rubbed his hand over his five o'clock shadowed chin as if thinking about something.

"Has the article gone to print yet?" he asked.

"It will print early tomorrow morning. Why?" Danika asked.

"Can you stop it?"

"Why do I need to stop it? I'm tired of everyone telling me what I can and can't print!"

"Please…! I'm not trying to tell you what you can print. I would just like to see what all it reveals before printing it.

"What would a picture reveal that could be so dangerous?" Danika asked as they proceeded on to the elevator.

"You mean your ex didn't explain that part to you?" Rob smirked. "Evidently you are still on friendly terms with him if he is helping you determine what goes into your magazine."

"Well…," Danika could feel her cheeks blushing, just thinking about the weekend. "He just came to my place this weekend while I was working on the magazine layout, to discuss our daughter and her new baby that is due in a couple of months." She bit her lip the instant the words flowed over her tongue. She wasn't very crazy about anyone, especially a good looking man like the one walking beside her, to know that she was about to become a grandma.

Danika sucked in a deep breath. "Okay! Enough said about my ex. Let's get this over with."

Agent Carson started laughing. "Am I that disgusting to you? Usually I don't have to argue with a woman when I ask her out for a cup of coffee."

"No…! Not really," Danika gave him a sheepish smile. "You just ask too many questions that aren't any of your business."

Once more Agent Carson took ahold of her elbow and directed her on to the elevator. The ride to the ground level was quiet as he seemed very deep in thought, and so was Danika. This meant that she was going to have to call Josh right away so that he didn't start the printing process before she got to work in the morning. It also meant that the magazine was going to be coming out to the public a couple days late while they re-organized its interior.

Once they were at the coffee shop, Agent Carson ordered coffee for the two of them while she called Josh at work and told him to pull the pictures and article written by Marty Vineteri. She knew by his hesitation that he felt she had lost her mind, but he didn't ask any questions. "I'll be in early and we will go over everything. Okay?" Danika tried smoothing it over before hanging up.

"Do you like pie?" Agent Carson asked.

Danika nodded her head and said, "I don't usually order it though."

"They make a killer apple pie here. Do you want to try it?"

"Am I going to need it?"

"You just never know what the future holds, so why not live a little dangerously, like eating some dessert that's loaded with calories for a change?"

"Is that the way you live your life?" Danika asked.

"My life's always in danger," Agent Carson grinned. "So, if I feel the need to eat a piece of pie or chocolate layered cake, I do it, just because tomorrow may never come and then I will have missed out on enjoying it."

His smile was contagious and growing on Danika and she found herself laughing and agreeing with his way of thinking, so he ordered a piece of apple pie Al-A-Mode for them both. And when it arrived with the coffee, she was surprised that it tasted so good to her. She just never ate things with a lot of calories, because she wanted to maintain her thirty year old looking figure. But in the back of her mind, becoming a Grandma meant that she was going to lose that figure. And whether she wanted to admit it or not, she enjoyed having good looking men such as Agent Carson finding her attractive. And now that he knew she was about to become a Grandmother, would he still feel the same? She doubted it!

Danika enjoyed the pie and the conversation that she was having with Agent Carson. He had given up asking her questions concerning Marty Vineteri and was asking her questions about herself that she didn't mind answering. He asked her all about Jani and the new baby that she was expecting, and even though Danika wasn't much in favor of talking about the new baby, the way he asked about it made the fact not quite so disturbing. Besides, she didn't want to admit to him about the way that she felt about the situation. He seemed to be one of those few men that she didn't have to psych herself up to be sure she was on the same plateau with. Talking to him was relaxing and enjoyable and not at all like so many corporate men that she was acquainted with. Too many of them that she had met with for lunch or coffee throughout her career acted like they thought they were above her level and it was maddening.

"Are you married?" she asked.

"Was! Not now," he flashed a surprised smile.

"Do you have any children?"

"Two!" The grin on his square face made her in the mind of the comic book figure, Dick Tracy. Yet his personality made her in the mind of Detective Columbo, a detective that she remembered watching on television with her parents' years before, and she just had to smile at the thought of the combination.

"Two? Two what?" she asked.

"I have a daughter that won't have anything to do with me and a son that just left home a couple of years ago when he decided to get married."

"What's up with the daughter?" Danika asked.

"Now who's doing the interrogating?" he continued to grin. "My ex-wife spread her bitterness about me onto our daughter after we broke up. Since my son chose to live with me, he and I get along just fine." Then he turned real serious. "I guess it wouldn't hurt so bad about not having contact with my daughter, but my ex won't even let her have any gifts or anything that I send to her. She returns everything but the money that she receives every month for child support. And because my son chose to live with me, his mother doesn't want anything to do with him, either. And my daughter feels the same way."

"I'm so sorry," Danika sympathized. "I can't imagine what it would be like to be rejected by your child. Why is your wife so bitter?"

"A lot of things! She didn't like the type of work that I do. She felt insecure and that made her constantly question what I was doing when I would stay out late at night working on a case or got called out of town. She would never believe me, so we were constantly fighting."

Danika just shook her head. "It was just the opposite for me," she retorted. "I trusted my husband too much and assumed that just because I wasn't cheating, neither was he. Boy was I wrong!"

Agent Carson really laughed. "Well Danika, it appears that we have a lot in common."

"I guess it does in a peculiar sort of way," she replied.

When the pie and coffee were gone, Agent Carson asked, "Do you mind showing me the pictures that Marty Vineteri took?"

"Why? The pictures and article just show the estate of Emanuel Vasquez and tells a little bit about his company that he moved to Des Moines. I don't know what they could possibly reveal that is of any importance to you."

"I'll be the judge of that," he scowled. "Besides, if I don't find anything suspicious, then you can go ahead and print the article and you won't have to hold anything up."

Danika glanced at her watch and decided that maybe if they hurried, she had time to take him back to the office to show him the pictures and still have time to make it to the Y to get in on the last bout of racquet ball with the girls.

"I guess!" she conceded.

Once again, she was wishing she had on decent shoes instead of her four inch Stilettos that she wore to work every day. They were fine as long as she was sitting at her desk. But doing a lot of walking in them, especially trying to keep up with the long strides of the man walking beside her was pure torture after having them on all day.

The security guard nodded at the same time he raised his eyebrows in question when Danika and Agent Carson re-entered the building. There wasn't much activity inside the building, as just about everyone had left for the day.

"I just need to show Agent Carson a couple of things in my office," Danika tried explaining to the guard. But she knew by the crooked smile that he gave her that he surmised she was going to show the man something alright, and he didn't figure it pertained to work! The thought of it made her blush and she could feel the heat rise up her neck and into her cheeks. The ride up the elevator to her suite was quiet, and she couldn't help but wonder if the same thing that was running through her head was also running through the head of the man standing next to her?

No Way! He was just doing his job! He couldn't possibly be interested in her! Besides, she wasn't interested in him, now that Ken was wanting back into her life. But then, she wasn't sure why Ken wanted back into her life after all these years, either.

Danika took Agent Carson straight to the production room where the manuscript pages of the magazine still laid sprawled out in numerical order on the huge work table. She picked out the picture of Emanuel Vasquez's estate and handed it to him, plus the short story that went with it. He looked at the picture, read the article, and then studied the picture again.

"May I have this?" he asked.

"Why?"

"Something tells me that there is more to this picture than what meets the ordinary eye. Maybe I'm just being skeptical."

"I suppose you want the article, too?" Danika scowled.

"Well," he grinned, "the article isn't much good without the picture is it?"

"I suppose you are right!" As much as Danika hated to admit it, she knew he was right, and the fact that both he and Ken thought it best the whole article be pulled made her feel terribly uncomfortable about the whole thing.

Agent Carson escorted Danika back out to her car, and she was almost depressed that their meeting had ended so shortly without any interest shown to her on his part.

"Danika!" It was Ken's voice on the other end of her cell phone again, and he sounded upset about something. "I was right! You know when I said I knew that biker from somewhere? Well, after digging in to past photos and records, I realized who he is, and that he has never been actually found guilty of it, but we all surmise that he is a hit man for the Mafia. He shows up and then disappears like a bad dream. And usually when he does, somebody gets killed. You have got to pull that article and that's all there is to it!"

"Relax," Danika started laughing. "The FBI has already confiscated the picture and the article."

"When?"

"This afternoon after I got off work."

"Where are you now?"

"I'm at the Y playing racquet ball with the girls."

"You be careful. Do you hear me?"

"Stop worrying Ken. I've got along without you for the past ten years and I can still do it. No one is going to bother me about anything. I haven't done anything."

"Do you know who he is?"

"Yes! Agent Carson told me all about him, and I've told my production crew not to allow any more articles from him. So, are you satisfied now?"

"How did the FBI know to come to you for the article?"

"They thought he worked for me and said they were trying to pin him for smuggling drugs. That's all I know."

Ken heaved a deep sigh. "Okay. Keep in contact, okay?"

"Yes, Ken! Stop worrying about me and keep concentrating on being a grandpa. Okay?"

"How can I not worry about you after this past couple of days? I have more to worry about than just becoming a grandpa."

Danika cringed. She didn't want to think about what may have happened during the past couple of nights that she had spent in bed with him.

"I have to go, Ken," she hurriedly changed the subject. "The girls are waiting for me to play another game."

"Is something wrong?" Marla asked as Danika tucked her cell phone back in her bra pocket again.

"No," Danika lied.

"I'm sorry! But I couldn't help but over hear the conversation. Were you talking to Ken?"

Danika nodded her head.

"Please tell me you two aren't trying to get back together again after all that he put you through."

"Why?"

By then Felisha and Alma were joining them.

"Who and whom are trying to get back together again?" Felisha asked. "Is there some juicy gossip that you need to be sharing with us?"

"Yes!" Marla scowled. "Our friend and her ex are thinking of getting back together again."

"I didn't say that!" Danika tried defending herself.

"You didn't have to!" Marla continued to frown. "You didn't deny it and your face is red."

"Really?" Felisha and Alma asked in unison.

"When did this happen?" Alma asked.

"I didn't say anything happened!" Danika continued trying to explain. "Except…except…, Jani informed us that she is expecting and Ken and I just got together over the weekend to discuss it. That's all!"

"You're going to be a grandma?" Felisha howled with glee. "That's great! When were you planning on telling us?"

"When did you find out?" Alma chimed in.

"Just a couple of days ago," Danika replied.

"And you didn't call us right away to tell us?" Marla scolded.

"What's so great about being a grandma?" Danika tried to brush the conversation aside by shrugging her shoulders.

"I can't believe you didn't call us immediately to tell us," Alma shook her head. "Shame on you!"

"That's great!" Felisha chortled again.

"When is she due?" Marla asked.

The flood of questions started being thrown at Danika one right after another and so fast by her three friends, that she had all she could do to answer any of them. Why couldn't she feel as excited about becoming a grandmother as everyone around her seemed to be? It was all so over whelming and disgusting. She bet if the tables were turned and it was one of *them*, they wouldn't be any happier about it than she was. The only thing good about all the questions was the fact that it took their interest away from talking about her and Ken. And she was glad that Marla hadn't picked up on the fact that the FBI had visited her at work today, because she absolutely didn't want to talk about that issue.

CHAPTER NINE

Danika did her usual routine in the morning before going to work. Thoughts of what all she had to do at work for the day were running through her head. She supposed she had better work with Josh to get the manuscript for the magazine put in order and sent off to the printing department. She hadn't heard anything more from Ken after she had told him that the FBI had pulled the article, and down deep inside, that bothered her. Past memories kept flooding her mind. Did she or did she not want to get back together with him? Could she or could she not trust him? Why's and whatnot's kept her mind occupied during her whole trip to the office. The past few days were like a bad dream that kept reappearing over and over.

"That FBI guy is waiting for you in your office again," Tara whispered when Danika reached her office.

"Did he say what he needed this time?" Danika scowled. She didn't need any more interruptions from the FBI. She just wanted to get the magazine printed and back to normal routine.

Tara shook her head. "He just asked if he could wait in your office until you got here."

"How long has he been here?" Danika asked.

Tara glanced at her watch. "Only about ten minutes."

Danika heaved a deep breath and shook her head. "Okay! Here goes!"

Tara just grinned at her boss' hesitation. It was so unlike Danika. In fact the whole past week her boss had been acting strange.

"May I help you Agent Carson?" Danika asked as she entered the room and closed the door. Once more he was standing at the window just watching all the activity out in the city below.

A big grin creased his face. "You can call me Beau."

"Okay, Beau. What brings you back this morning?"

"I had a chance to study the picture better and also our forensic scientist studied it. We think that your man Vineteri has been using your magazine to send messages. We just don't know who too or for sure what the message is. But you can bet that whoever it is knows that the article should be coming out in tomorrow's edition."

"So?"

"So, someone is going to wonder where it is when it doesn't appear."

"I don't understand what that has to do with me," Danika frowned.

"What don't you understand? Whoever it is intended for may come looking for it either here or your place."

A pang of fear hit Danika like a bolt of lightning. Ken had said that Marty was a hit man for the Mafia.

"Then you better bring it back so no one suspects that you have it"

"Can't do that," he shook his head.

"Don't you care about the danger you have just subjected me and my employees to?"

"Yes! That's why I'm here."

"I know you came to warn me, but what can I do about it? I can't just shut the place down so we all stay safe."

"I realize that," Agent Carson sounded sympathetic. "I'm here to ask you to let one of our agents stay with you for a while until we can get more information."

"No!" Danika scowled. "I am not going to be subjected to that kind of attention. It will scare all of my friends and resources away. It's hard enough trying to find articles to go in the magazine without you trashing it."

"Okay," Agent Carson frowned. "I can see that arguing with you is going to get me nowhere. Don't say I didn't warn you. I would think that you would want to think of your daughter and how she would feel if you didn't get to see your first grandchild!"

"Thank you for your concern. But I will be okay. If I see anyone snooping around, I will let you know," Danika forced a smile.

"Believe me when I say that you will never see what might hit you."

"If that's the case, then having one of your agents for a shadow won't make much difference then, will it?"

Agent Carson just shook his head in disbelief. "You are something else. Do you know that? Anyone else would be thankful for the information and the offer to give you a shadow for your own safety. Our department doesn't have that many agents to spare, so when we offer, we know that it's a dire need and not just for the fun of it!"

"I thank you and I appreciate the offer. But I can't stop living my normal life just because some nut wants to end it. I'll take my chances."

"In that case then, would you be interested in having dinner with me tonight?" Beau asked.

"I'm sorry," Danika apologized. "But I have a ton of things to do tonight."

"Like what?" he didn't conceal his disappointment very well.

Why couldn't she and why was she so quick to reject the offer? Think of something quick!

"I suppose if we weren't out too late, I could," Danika heard herself saying. "I'll just have to do everything when I get home."

"Great!" A huge pleased smile creased his face again. "I'll pick you up about 7:00. Will that work?"

"I guess." For the life of her, Danika couldn't figure out why all of a sudden she was feeling like a giddish school girl inside again. Who was this man and why was she excited about being invited out to dinner with him? After all, she had been asked out hundreds of times by men, and they always ended up being just another man whom she wasn't interested in, or cared to be associated with unless it was business. But the thought of sitting across the table with this man again, just to have a comfortable, enjoyable and relaxing time, sounded very appealing to her. Maybe it was because she knew she could just be herself and not someone who had to talk up politics or what was going on in the stock market. Most of the time she didn't worry about what the stock market prices were doing in the daily NASDAC or DOW JONES on Wall Street. She just worried about her own company and knew it didn't have any stocks on the market to watch fluctuate. She just watched the profit margin that her company was or wasn't making.

After he left the room, she wished she had asked where he was taking her, so she knew how to dress. But, his invitation had taken her so by surprise that she hadn't really given it the proper thought. And come to think about it, he hadn't asked for her phone number or her address, which meant that he already had it. And that was scary! Who else knew where she lived?

The more she thought about what he had told her, the more she could feel the fear creeping into her whole being, which was so unlike her. And the more the fear creped in, the more she wished she could just go home, curl up with a good book and drink another bottle of Merlot and forget this whole past week had ever existed. Maybe Ken was right! Maybe she *was* becoming dependent on the wine and needed the AAA meetings. She could feel the fear, but didn't realize how much of it she had encountered until Josh's voice paging her over the intercom made her jump so high that she almost fell off her chair.

"I'm ready to rejuvenate the manuscript, Ma'am. Do you want to help or do you want me to ask someone else?"

"I'll be right there." She was actually glad for the opportunity to put her mind to work doing something worthwhile on the manuscript instead of worrying about her sordid life right now.

Beau Carson was ringing the outdoor buzzer right on time, and Danika checked her form in the floor length hall mirror, making sure her two piece peplin dress looked okay. It was a silky white lace top with a black skirt and one that she had purchased to wear just for such an occasion when she wasn't expected to be wearing a business suit or a fancy cocktail dress. A large black and white beaded necklace circled her neck and the matching earrings sparkled under her long hair. Her black with white toed matching stilettos finished the look. She guessed she would do. After all, he was anything but perfect in his black war torn suit that he had been wearing every time he was in her office. He had actually looked a little scruffy both times, so she worried that she might be overdressed for the occasion tonight.

What she saw when she opened the door shocked her. Instead of wearing the suit that she had expected him to be dressed in, he was dressed in a black knit Henley polo shirt and a nice pair of kaki dress slacks with a black belt. And the short sleeve knit shirt exposed every taunt, bulging, muscle that his whole torso and arms were made up of. There could not have been one ounce of fat on the man. Along with being surprised with how he was dressed, she couldn't help but inhale the sexy smelling aura that emanated all around him. As her eyes combed over him, she realized that he was doing the same thing to her, and she suddenly felt conspicuous and at a loss of words as the flushing heat rushed into her cheeks. *This was definitely not what she was expecting!*

"Are you ready?" His smile was catching and his voice was tender when he spoke, sending her further into another realm of space, causing her brain to take another couple of seconds to actually absorb what he was asking. *Earth to Danika!*

"Uhhhh...! Just as soon as I grab my purse," she finally answered. She held the door so he could step in to wait on her while she hurried to the den to grab her small black evening bag that she had put together earlier for the occasion.

"Nice place!" he remarked as she returned back to where he was standing, still in front of the door, just looking around.

"Thanks! It's just the right size for someone living alone," she smiled. Why she said that, she had no idea, and why she was suddenly nervous about the whole situation was beyond her comprehension. Maybe it was because this was the first actual date that a man had come calling for her at her apartment since she and Ken had divorced. She had always met them somewhere like a fancy restaurant or one of the country clubs on all the other dates she had encountered.

What surprised her even more than the way Beau was dressed, was the car that he was driving. It was a Black Mazda sports convertible, and he had the top down on it.

"Do you mind riding in a convertible or do you want the top up?" he asked as he held the door open for her.

"I don't mind at all," she grinned. "I haven't ridden in a convertible since I was a teenager!"

"I'll take my time so you don't get all windblown tonight. You look so nice; I would hate to ruin it."

Danika was proud to be riding with him in this car. Not only because the car was drawing attention. But because when you got right down to it, she was riding with a pretty handsome man, and she knew that as long as she was with him, she wouldn't be in any danger.

"Do You like Italian food?" he asked.

"I love Italian!" she answered.

"Italian it is then," he smiled.

He took her across town to Carrabba's, and Danika was surprised when they were escorted right past a crowd that was standing waiting to be seated at a table.

"Right this way, Mr. Carson," the hostess said when he gave her his name.

She took them to a small table set up with an ice bucket and bottle of wine in it, plus as soon as she had seated them, she lit the candle in the middle of the table, and then she unscrewed the cork on the top of a wine bottle and filled the two crystal goblets.

"Your waitress is Holly and she will be here to take your order in just a few minutes. Enjoy your meal." With that the hostess walked away, leaving the two of them alone in a very romantic atmosphere.

"Wow!" Danika grinned. "How did you manage this?"

"I believe it is called using your cell phone," he teased.

"What if I had said no to the Italian food?"

"I guess I would have crossed that bridge when I got to it if it happened. But I didn't expect you to turn your nose up at anything I suggested. According to your magazine, the chief editor likes to eat at about every restaurant in town. And I think she has even done some articles on fancy restaurants in places like Chicago and New York, to name a few."

"You have definitely done your homework! Haven't you?" Danika grinned.

"I try!"

His smile was salacious and she caught it, making her squirm a little in her chair. *Was she ready for something like this?* She didn't get a chance to think about it further, because Holly was there to take their order. After Holly left them alone again, Danika took a sip of wine. She didn't know what kind it was for sure, but it was so mellow and sweet that one sip called for another, and before she knew it, she was starting to feel the buzz of it. She had gone all day without eating except the bagel and yogurt for breakfast, and now she was sorry for skipping lunch. The food couldn't get there fast enough. Of all people, she didn't want the evening to be impaired in front of this man by her drinking.

Danika found herself really enjoying the meal and the time being spent with Beau. He was so easy to talk to, and she realized she was laughing at just about everything he said, like a young silly teenager. Every time their eyes connected, she saw the ardent smiles he was sending her way, and each time it felt like a whole colony of butterflies were flapping their wings inside her stomach. She couldn't remember the last time she had felt this way, and that alone made her all the more nervous.

Being nervous at a meal just wasn't her style. Her mother had made sure that Danika knew her etiquette while growing up. "Just in case my beautiful daughter ever gets to eat with royalty," she used to say when Danika would object to taking the classes that her mom insisted on. And ever since Danika had started her own magazine, she had thanked her mother over a zillion times for forcing her to learn which fork was proper to use at which time, how to place a napkin on her lap properly, how to hold the pinkie finger while picking up a tea cup, and never, never letting her elbows rest on the table, or picking her teeth, no matter how much food was stuck in them. Now if she could just have a chance to curtsy to a royal debutante somewhere, she felt her schooling would be complete.

It had always been her dream to actually get to use all that etiquette training sometime by being invited to attend a real royal affair somewhere. She didn't care if it was the first lady of France, the princess of Monaco, or the king of Saudi Arabia; she just wanted to be able to tell her grandchildren someday that she had sat down with royalty somewhere instead of just staying overnight in the Cinderella suite at Disney World.

And then it hit her! She was about to be receiving that grandchild and she had never attended a royal meal anywhere. Hmmmm! Maybe by the time she turned eighty, she would have the chance. After all, that's when grandmas sat their little ones on their laps to tell them bedtime stories. Not now, when she was this age. Maybe there was time yet!

"I suppose I had better get you home so you can get done what you had to do tonight," Beau said when they had finished their four course meal and the bottle of wine.

Danika glanced at her watch, acting like she agreed with him, when in actuality; she really wasn't in that big of a hurry to part company with him. He had made her evening so enjoyable that she had forgotten all about her woes of the past week.

Beau took Danika home and walked her to her apartment door. *Was he going to try to kiss her? Should she invite him in? Did he like her well enough to ask her out again?* So many things were running through her head. Right before she stuck the key into the knob, Beau said, "I have a couple of tickets to see Mama Mia at the Civic Center tomorrow night. Would you like to go with me to see it?"

"Are you serious?" Danika grinned. She knew the live show was coming to the center, but when she had mentioned it to the girls, they each had other things to do or had already seen it, and the play was only going to be in Des Moines two weeks. "I would like that!" *And I would love to spend another night with you*! The words raced through her head but stopped before they escaped her lips. She had to literally scold herself inside for feeling so excited about the invitation and not letting herself sound so anxious.

"Great!" Beau replied. "I'll pick you up about six so we have time to eat before we go to the center. Will that work?"

Danika nodded, knowing that she probably looked overly zealous about the whole thing.

"Thanks for the meal and good time tonight," she said as Beau turned to walk toward the elevator to go home.

He stopped and turned around and gave her two thumbs up and another salacious smile and said, "Until tomorrow night!" And then he stepped on the elevator and was gone. For some reason, Danika felt a huge pang of disappointment. He was gone and he hadn't even tried to kiss her goodnight. She inhaled a deep breath and then took her time sticking the key into the keyhole to unlock the door.

But she stopped just before turning the knob because the door to the escape stairwell opened and a black male in his middle thirties stepped out into the hall.

He stopped when he saw Danika, gave her a slight nod and then walked on down the hall and on around the corner. His head was shaven, his arms were covered with tattoos, and he had on a muscle T-shirt with faded blue jeans. Not the sort of person that should be visiting anyone in her building. She pretty much knew everyone that lived on her floor, and he didn't fit in. Hmmmm! Was she being paranoid again? She hurriedly turned the knob and slammed the door behind her, locking it immediately before even turning on the lights.

To add to her already aberrant state of mind, her cell phone rang in her clutch purse. Her hands were shaking so bad, she had trouble getting the purse unzipped and the phone out before it quit. But the number flashed across the screen told her that it was Ken.

Ken! She had spent the entire evening without giving him a thought. What was up with that?

Danika slowly made her way going from room to room, turning on all the lights as she did so, just to ensure that the place was free of any intruder and hadn't been ram-sacked while she was gone. When she felt safe, she went back to the kitchen and was just pressing the button on the Keurig for a cup of coffee when her phone rang again.

"Hey girl, where have you been?" Ken asked.

"I had dinner with a client," Danika lied. "Why?"

"I've been trying to call you and when you weren't answering your home phone or your cell phone, I was beginning to get worried."

"If I remember right," Danika frowned, "your calling me constantly was part of the reason we ended up in a divorce."

"If I remember right, your life wasn't in danger before we got our divorce!"

"No one says my life is in danger now, either," she argued, even though she knew better.

"You and I both know it could be. Have you heard anything from the FBI since they confiscated the article?"

"Not much!" Danika answered.

"What do you mean by 'not much'?"

"For Pete's sake, Ken! Will you just stop worrying? I'm going to be okay."

"How did your test result turn out?" he asked.

"What test?" Danika scowled. What in the world was he talking about? She hadn't taken any test.

"You know? After the weekend! Are you or aren't you?"

It took Danika a second to realize what test he was talking about, before she answered, "I haven't had time to even think about it or get to a drug store to purchase it. I will before the week is up. Okay?"

That seemed to satisfy Ken even though he clearly expressed his disappointment that she hadn't already done so. *Was he anxious because he wanted to be a new daddy again? Or was he anxious because he didn't want to be a new daddy again? How Danika wished she knew what was running through his head.* He changed the subject to asking if she had heard anything more from Jani. She hadn't and neither had he.

"Do you have a lot going on tomorrow?" he asked.

"Yes! I have a couple of appointments and then I'm going to the Civic Center with the girls to see Mama Mia. Why?" Danika lied again.

"I have a couple of tickets to go see Mama Mia tomorrow night too, and I wanted you to go with me!'

"Why didn't you say something before you bought the tickets?" Danika scolded.

"I wanted to surprise you with them. I just picked them up this afternoon."

Danika's heart sank! How did she get herself out of this one? If Ken took someone else, he would see her with Beau Carson instead of the girls. And if she cancelled with Beau and went with Ken, he would know that she had been lying about it in the first place. If she played sick and didn't go with either one, she would miss the play altogether, and she didn't want that either.

"I'm sorry. If I had known, I wouldn't have told the girls that I would go with them," Danika tried to get herself around the situation. But the more she tried to lie herself out of it, the more it called for another lie, and since lying was something she wasn't good at, it seemed her mind was going blank and no more words wanted to come across her tongue.

"I'll just have to see if someone at the office can use them or wants to go with me." Ken sounded so disappointed, that Danika almost felt sorry for him. "So, I guess I'll just have to see what happens. Maybe I'll see you there, and maybe I won't."

Even though Danika wished him luck with the situation before he hung up, she knew that she was the one that needed the luck to get out of the situation she had just placed herself into.

As luck had it, Beau took her to the Latin King for dinner, and the restaurant was so busy that by the time they were done eating, it was time for the play to start, and by the time they reached the Civic Center, the crowded lobby had cleared out and people were already filing in to find their assigned seats. Hopefully, Ken would be busy enough finding his seat that he wouldn't notice her coming in. However, she didn't want to take a chance, so she asked Beau for her ticket with the excuse that she had to visit the ladies room and would find him just as soon as she was done.

"Do you know this place well enough to find your seat?" he questioned.

Danika nodded her head and hurried down the hall to the restroom. She knew that once it was time for the play to start, the lights to the seating area would be shut off and no one would see her, except the usher, and he would direct her with his flashlight. And she was right. So until intermission time, she knew she was safe, and she would just stay put during intermission instead of getting up to get something to drink or to go to the restroom again. Her only concern now was that their seats were in the middle of the seating arena, and she had no idea if Ken would be behind her or in front of her. Maybe if she crossed her fingers, he would be seated in front of her. But then, since he had just purchased the tickets the day before, it was likely that he would be towards the back.

The play was awesome and just what she expected it to be. It was light hearted and entertaining, and at the same time it left an impression on her heart and soul. She had grown up loving music sang by ABBA, so the live play brought back so many memories for her, like memories of some of the things she and Ken had done together while they were dating, and then some of the heartaches that followed. She never dreamed that they would someday be going separate ways. Nor had she ever thought about becoming a grandma. She had thought about having children, but not any further than that. Now she was living a life that she had virtually never dreamed of or surmised could even happen. It had been filled with all kinds of twists and turns that she had never suspected.

Beau offered to buy her a glass of wine to drink during intermission, but she refused. She didn't know what else to do. She didn't want him to know why, and at the same time she couldn't take a chance of being spotted by Ken.

She stayed seated while Beau left to go to the restroom, and then she spied Ken setting five rows in front of her, and wished she hadn't, because he was with a nice looking woman that was probably in her late thirties or early forties. She had long hair, was brunette and just from what little Danika could see from behind, she probably had a very nice figure of maybe a size four or five, and Ken seemed to be very pleased to be in her company, as did she to be with him. How dare he? He had accused Danika of being the same old person she had been before, when in essence; he was the same old Ken. Leave it to him to go searching for another good looking female when she wasn't available. She had just made up her mind to go confront him and introduce herself to his date when Beau slid in the seat next to her. *Maybe she would do it later. But, not right now.* Confronting Ken would have to be at a later date. Now to be able to leave without her being seen with Beau would take some more scheming.

Saved by the unwanted grace of Rosetta Dunfee! "Danika, darling!" The petite, redheaded woman grabbed Danika's arm as

Danika passed by, taking Danika completely off guard and almost relieved, at the same time. "How are you?"

"I..., I'm doing great! Thank you," Danika responded with a sigh of relief in her voice as the crowd continued to move around her and Beau.

"I hear your magazine has been doing some fine articles these days," Rosetta gave Danika a factious smile at the same time she let her eyes comb over Beau as if just waiting to start some juicy gossip about who Danika was with.

"Yes!" Danika returned the smile. "And I hear you are still working for the Meredith Corporation and still setting at the same desk." Why she wanted to get that dig in there, Danika didn't know, but it felt good, because she had never had the chance to retaliate after Rosetta had spread the gossip that Danika had been fired from Meredith and that was why she had went out and started her own company with her late daddy's money.

"At least I still know I have a pay check coming each week!" Rosetta sneered. "I hear your company has been facing some tough times lately. What a shame it would be if you had to close your doors."

Danika started frowning. "I'm not sure where you heard your information, but my company is doing just fine, thank you very much!" With that she took ahold of Beau's arm and turned to finish walking with the heavy flow of the crowd to the door. *How dare Rosetta make such an insinuation?*

Danika and Beau were almost to the exit door shuffling along with the people that were filing outside when she heard her name, and it was Ken's voice. Damn! Her heart sank! Now what was she to do? Maybe just ignore it and act like she didn't hear it? Yes! That was exactly what she did. But, Beau heard it too, and taking ahold of her arm he stopped her and said, "I think someone over there is calling your name."

"Really?" Danika faked a surprise.

"Yes," Beau replied. "There's a man's voice on the other side of the lobby calling out your name."

Trying to stop midstream the heavy flow of traffic filing out was almost impossible, so Danika proceeded on out the door.

"I guess we can wait here and see who it is," she said as they stepped on outside.

The night was warm and pretty under the street lights, so waiting for Ken to catch up with them wasn't as bad as it could have been. Having Beau standing next to her had a calming effect on her too, although she hadn't figured out how she was going to explain to Ken why she was with him instead of her best friends.

Finally Ken and his date came through the door and made their way through the crowd that was now gathered outside either standing, talking, or hurrying to their cars and the buses to leave.

"I tried getting your attention in the lobby," Ken said. "But I guess you couldn't hear me above the noise of the crowd."

"Agent Carson heard you, but we would have gotten trampled if we had tried stopping in there," Danika replied.

"Agent Carson?" A frown creased Ken's face.

"Yes!" Beau stuck his hand out. "I'm Danika's escort tonight."

"But I thought you said you were coming with the girls!" Ken continued to frown.

"I had planned on it, but Agent Carson thinks I should have a body guard with me at all times now!"

"Why?" Ken asked Beau.

Before Beau could respond, Danika said, "This isn't the place to be discussing anything, Ken. What did you want with me?" She glanced at the woman still standing silently beside Ken's side, holding on to his arm with both of her hands, while leaning first on one foot and then the other, as if her feet were hurting her, or else she was completely bored with the whole scenario. Whatever the reason, she was just as good looking and her figure was to die for, as Danika had suspected. *She* could keep right on being trim and neat, without her age being announced to the whole world about becoming a grandma. And by the way she was grasping Ken's arm, Danika knew that she was going to be readily available to make him happy tonight and as many more as he needed. Danika felt sick inside. If he knew what was good for him, the test she was going to take tomorrow had better be negative, because she wasn't going to be bound to him as long as he had a female like this one standing by trying to get his attention.

"Oh!" Ken finally grinned and shook Beau's still outstretched hand. "I wanted you to meet our newest member in the DA's office. Lauren Devilbiss, meet my ex-wife, Danika Bronson."

Lauren nodded to Danika and Beau, refusing Danika's offer to shake hands.

"I'm pleased to meet you, Lauren," Danika lied. "What do you do at the office?"

"I'm an assistant district attorney," Lauren pursed her lips in a sneering smile.

"Great!" Danika replied. "So does that mean Ken won't be tied down there as much as he has been?"

"It means that we will be working together so we can handle more cases at one time," Lauren replied in her same repugnant tone.

"Hopefully it won't take so long to get a case ready for trial now," Ken added. "Now if we could just get the court system to do the same, we wouldn't have such a back log."

"Well Lauren," Danika forced a smile over gritted teeth, "good luck in your new position. I'm sure that Ken needs your help, since he will be slowing down a little bit now that he is about to become a grandpa. However, I'm sure you and Ken will do just fine working together. In fact, I can almost guarantee that before long, you'll be more to him than just an assistant and you will be getting some extra benefits with your new position."

Lauren scowled and gave her head a short nod as if trying to understand just what Danika was getting at. However, a frown creased Ken's face again. He knew exactly what Danika meant with her salutation.

"It was nice meeting you," Danika continued. And then she looked at Beau, and said, "I suppose we had better go, don't you think? It's getting late."

"I'll be calling you so you can explain what's going on," Ken called after them as they turned to walk away.

Danika just raised her hand and waved it over her shoulder without turning back to respond.

"What was that all about?" Beau asked when they got further away from the hub of people still standing in front of the theater.

"I'm sorry for what just happened. I'm not sure what it is," Danika shook her head. "I don't think I'm jealous. I guess I'm still bitter. Seeing him with another female like her just brings back too many old memories. He likes his women sharp, sexy, and good looking. And the fact that he went out of his way to introduce her to me sends up a warning flag."

Beau started laughing.

"What?" Danika failed to see any humor in it.

"All men like women that are sharp, sexy and good looking. And some of us even like them to be intelligent and likeable!"

"Point being what?"

"Just that! I think he went out of his way to introduce you to her tonight because he is still in love with you and deliberately wanted to make you jealous. It is easy to see that he still cares about you."

"He sure has a funny way of showing it!" Danika snipped. She had so many things running through her head about the whole situation. She knew Ken well enough to know that he was going to find someone to have sex with, one way or another. If it wasn't her, it would be with someone like Lauren. And if he was still in love with her, why would he try hurting her again by going out of his way to introduce her to someone as good looking as Lauren? Surely there was someone else in that office that he could have given the tickets to or brought along with him tonight since he knew that he would be seeing her there with the girls.

The only conversation during the drive to her apartment was only about the cast of Mama Mia, and how much they had enjoyed the show. Beau didn't ask any questions or suggest any more conversation that had to do with what had happened with Ken after the play was over, and for that, Danika was grateful.

"Since I'm just here to keep you safe, I guess I had better walk you all the way up to your floor to be sure you stay that way," Beau grinned when they reached the apartment building.

"I'm sorry! I know what it sounded like back there and I didn't mean for it to come off that way," Danika tried explaining. "You had already asked me to go to the play and when Ken called and asked me to go with him; I had to think of something quick. I know how he can be if he thinks I'm not telling him everything. And I know now that he won't give me any rest until this whole thing is over with. Even though he doesn't care enough to be faithful, he cares enough to worry about me."

"Some men are just like that," Beau replied. "They want to be able to have it all their way, and that's what gets a lot of them into trouble."

"I really enjoyed going to the play with you," Danika admitted, as they climbed out of the car.

"I guess I should feel honored that you kept your date with me instead of breaking it to keep him happy," Beau said as they unlocked the outside apartment door.

If he only knew what all had raced through her mind trying to decide how to keep both of them happy!

"Would you like to come in for a cup of coffee or a night cap before you leave?" Danika asked when they stepped off the elevator and walked down the hall to her apartment door.

"Coffee sounds good," Beau smiled.

"Coffee it is then!"

But when Danika went to unlock the door, it was already unlocked, and the knob turned much too easy.

"That's strange," she frowned. "I could have sworn I locked this door. I just never go out without locking it."

CHAPTER TEN

"Step back," Beau said as he reached inside his suit jacket and pulled a Glock pistol out of his shoulder holster. He slowly opened the door and reached in to flip the switch that turned the two living room lamps on.

"Oh my God!" Danika gasped. "What on earth happened?"

Someone had been in her apartment and ram-sacked everything in it. She stood frozen in her tracks as Beau slowly searched throughout the whole place, making sure no one was still in it. Danika didn't know whether to scream, start crying, or just stand there, trembling as she looked around at the horrible mess spewed in front of her. All she could think of was, who had been there, why would someone do this and what would have happened if she had been home alone?

"Do you believe me now?" Beau asked as he holstered his gun and walked back to where she still stood staring around in disbelief.

"Y…yes!" she managed to respond. "Do you really, seriously think they were looking for that article?"

"Yes," Beau answered. "Are you sure you haven't seen anyone strange lurking around? Who all knows where you live? Better yet, who knew which apartment was yours, and how did they get in here?"

Then Danika remembered the bald headed black man that had come through the stairwell door the night before and told Beau all about him.

"Why didn't you say something?" Beau scolded.

"I didn't think anything of it when he just nodded and walked on down the hall. I just thought maybe he was someone that was visiting the woman in the apartment down around the corner. He was young enough that he could have been a grandson." And then she remembered how that same little old lady had let Ken in to the apartment building because he had told her that he was Danika's brother. Had the intruder done the same thing?

"Do you think you could explain that young man to a sketch artist?"

"I can try," Danika agreed.

"Don't touch anything until we get the CSI in here to dust for fingerprints. Okay?"

"Can I make us that coffee, or do I have to wait?"

"Go ahead and make the coffee. Just try not to touch any cupboard knobs if possible, because so many things have been pulled out of the cupboards as well as all your closets, desks and everything that had drawers, including the china buffet. I'm sorry, but there's been a lot of breakage of things. Whoever did this was either desperate or just plain mean."

Beau started making calls as Danika tip-toed through the scrambled mess on the floor, all the way to the kitchen. She grabbed a paper towel off the roller and used it to get a couple of unbroken cups out of the cupboard. She didn't have to worry about touching any cupboard handles, because every door in the kitchen area was still open. Even the pans had been pulled out and thrown to the floor. And then she had a horrible thought! All of her pictures of Jani were hanging on the wall in the den! If fact, the wall was covered with them.

Danika stopped with the coffee and hurried through the mess, trying not to step on anything, and her heart sank when she saw where the pictures should have been hanging. Every one of the frames had been smashed and torn apart. Some of the pictures were still intact, but the brunt of them had been ripped. That was the last straw, and she couldn't contain the tears that were now flowing down her cheeks. Beau had followed her into the den, and gathered her in his arms, offering his shoulder when he saw how upset she was.

"Why?" she wailed. "Why would they rip up the pictures?"

"I imagine they were trying to see if you had anything hidden between the picture and the frame."

"Why would I do that?" Danika frowned. "What kind of animal destroyed all of this? If they would have used any common sense, they would have known that the article had to be at the office."

And then another thought hit her!

"Oh my God! Did they do anything at the magazine suite?"

"Let me make another call and see if there was any break in there. You have security guards there twenty four hours, don't you?" Beau asked.

Danika nodded her head and then her heart sank deeper when she saw the look on Beau's face as he completed his call.

"I'm sorry Danika, but yes, your suite was broken into. The security guard was shot and is in critical condition at the hospital."

"Why wasn't I notified?" she wailed louder.

"I don't know. Did you have your phone on?"

A frown creased Danika's face. "As a matter of fact, I shut it off before we entered the theater, and it is still off." She reached for the phone on the desk. Maybe they had tried calling her on that phone. It was the only thing on the top of the desk that was still intact. And when she reached for the phone, she realized that her laptop was missing. It wasn't on top of the desk or on the floor. It was gone. So many things were stored on that lap top and she hadn't done any backups. She had never dreamed that it could be stolen out of a secured apartment like hers.

By the time they had made their way through the whole apartment, accessing the damage, the city police had arrived. Danika was so embarrassed when they walked into her bedroom. Things like her red bikini panties, flowered bras, and black slip and nylon hosieries were strewn across the floor, and "oh no!" her precious state fair teddy bear had been ripped open, slashed right down the middle as if whoever done this thought she was talented enough to bury a secret message in the poor thing. Now what was she supposed to cuddle up to? She clutched the teddy bear to her bosom and wailed all the louder, not caring that Beau was scratching his head as if wondering if she was on the verge of insanity!

Not only had the laptop been stolen, but so had Danika's wooden jewelry box that Ken had given her on their first Christmas after they were married. Most of all her jewelry was expensive costume that had been purchased to match the outfits that she wore. Several items, like a couple of lockets and a diamond ring that had belonged to her mother, were also in that box. They were things that Danika had cherished and wanted to pass on down to Jani, and yes, even to her grand-daughter when the time was right. She guessed she should have had them secured in something besides a wooden box sitting on her dresser, but she wore the diamond ring a lot when she went to special occasions.

Danika gave the police a description of everything that had been stolen, and then Beau drove her downtown to see what damage had been done to her magazine company. Police were standing outside the building as well as her suite, guarding everything. Beau suspected that whoever had done all the damage to Danika's apartment and to the magazine offices had to be more than one person. Printing machines, laptops, computers, desks, and tables had been damaged. It appeared as if someone had gone in with sledge hammers and just busted up everything that stood in their path. And it was a sure thing that they were only interested in destroying what belonged to Danika, since no other offices or businesses in the building had been broken into or destroyed.

Danika's knees felt like they wanted to buckle out from under her when she looked around at all the devastation. They had suddenly turned to rubber and she had to find a wall to lean against to keep from slinking to the floor. A sickening nausea engulfed her whole being and she swore she was going to heave.

"Are you okay?" She could hear Beau asking, but his voice seemed to be miles away. "You look pretty pale!"

Danika tried nodding her head, but that just made the sickening feeling get worse. "I just need to sit down," she whispered.

Beau slipped his arm around her waist and helped her get to the nearest chair that hadn't been overturned. One hundred thoughts kept swirling through her head. She just knew that her career with the magazine was finished, plus she had to get ahold of all of the employees to let them know that they didn't have a job to come to the next day. She glanced at her watch and was even more surprised that it was now past midnight. She knew that no employee would appreciate being called out of bed at this time of the night just to be informed that they were no longer employed. The next thing was getting insurance adjusters in there and the apartment. She had both places insured against fire and acts of nature, but she wasn't sure how much coverage she had on both places for something as tragic as this. Where was Ken when she needed him? Probably in Laurens bed by now! Damn him any way! For two cents she should call him and tell him what had happened, just to interrupt the wild sex that she knew he was probably enjoying. And then Rosetta's words hit her! Did her office being destroyed have anything to do with Rosetta? Rosetta seemed to know that her company was going to have problems. But how?

"Where are you taking me?" Danika asked when Beau helped her into his car and informed her that she couldn't go back to her apartment to stay until they were all done investigating everything.

"To my place," he smiled.

"Do you take all your victims to your place in a situation like this?"

"Just the pretty ones," he teased.

"Do you have any wine?"

"Why? I thought we were going to have a cup of coffee."

"Yes. But now I think I need something stronger than coffee."

"I might be able to come up with something stronger than coffee for you. I won't guarantee that it will be wine, since I'm not much of a wine drinker."

Danika glanced through the dimness of only the passing street lights and the interior lights on the dash of the car, at the man driving her to where ever it was that he lived.

"You don't have to do this, you know. I can get a hotel room."

"I know I don't have to," he shot her a warm smile and then reached over and squeezed her hand. "I want to."

She pulled her hand away, and replied, "You aren't going to try to take advantage of a damsel in distress are you?"

Beau shook his head. "Not if she doesn't want me too. I might be a jerk sometimes, but I'm not stupid."

Beau lived in an urban part of Altoona. One would never suspect that he lived in such a nice middle class neighborhood, from his appearance while he was working. But when the garage door automatically opened and they pulled inside, Danika realized that he was just like every other working man on the block. His garage held all kinds of garden tools, a lawn mower, a set of golf bags, and all sorts of boxes that were stored on shelves, just like every typical urban garage.

The inside of his ranch style brick home was just as neat and clean as his garage. The furniture wasn't the highly expensive kind like her apartment held, but it was comfortable and cozy. Once they were inside, he showed her around, showing her both bedrooms, and explained that she was welcome to sleep on the davenport or in the bedroom that had previously belonged to his son.

"Make yourself at home while I go find you something to drink and make me a pot of coffee."

The first thing Danika headed for was the bathroom. She had forgotten all about the Sangria wine she had drank at the restaurant until now and suddenly it was pressing on her. A shower also sounded good. Just as soon as they shared their drinks, she was going to ask Beau if she could shower. It had been a long day and maybe a relaxing shower would help calm her down. But then she had a second thought! She didn't have any clothes to change into or put on. Not even in the morning, so she guessed the shower was out. Heaven forbid!

"Do you have a T-shirt or something I could wear to sleep in?" Danika asked as she sauntered into the kitchen.

"Sure! Actually, you can wear a pair of my PJs if you want."

Danika started grinning.

"What?" Beau asked when he saw the questioning look on her face.

"I just don't think of you as being a pajama kind of guy."

"Well, I wear the bottoms just in case I would have an emergency and need to evacuate my house during the middle of the night." Beau laughed. "I wouldn't want my neighbors seeing me naked."

"Ahhhhh!" Danika nodded her head and gave him an insidious giggle.

"Do you prefer beer or brandy?" Beau changed the subject.

"You mean I have a choice!" she asked.

"Sure! I'm right up town!"

"Well, I don't care much for beer, and I've never drank a brandy. So maybe I had better stick with the coffee." Danika replied.

"In that case, I'll pour you a sample of brandy to try. I keep it on hand just to warm me up when it's really cold or if I've had a really rough day."

He reached in his cupboard and pulled out a brandy sniffer, poured a small amount of brandy in it and handed it to her.

"Don't...!"

He spoke too late! Danika had already tipped it up and swallowed the whole sample.

"Oh my God!" she gasped through the choking that followed. She grabbed her throat first, and then her stomach. Tears welled up in her eyes, blinding her, and she couldn't stop them. Little had she been prepared for the burning sensation that engulfed her throat all the way to the pit of her stomach. "That's awful! Why does it burn so?"

"I'm sorry!" Beau flashed an amiable grin. "I tried to warn you that you were only supposed to sip it until you got used to it. Actually, it's pretty sweet, compared to bourbon."

"I don't drink bourbon, either!" Danika continued holding her throat.

"Would you like me to mix it with some 7-up or ice to weaken it?"

"No thanks!"

Danika didn't want him to think she was a big wimp, but she didn't want to try drinking that awful stuff again, no matter what it was mixed with. "I'll just settle for coffee."

"I'm really sorry!" Beau apologized again.

The tender look he gave Danika was mesmerizing, and before either one of them gave it much thought, they were in each other's arms and exchanging kisses. His kisses were tender and delectable--- just like tasting a piece of three layered dark chocolate cake smothered with creamy fudge frosting,--- and they were having a tremendous comforting effect on her. They were smoothing all the troubles out of her mind better than all the grape wine in California could have done. She didn't care that his hand started inching its way down to the small of her back, pulling her in tight against him, then on to the buttocks, then on to her thigh, and finally, carefully inched its way back up in under her dress. She just wanted those kisses to continue and not stop. And they did, all the way to the bedroom.

"You aren't going to need those pajamas," Beau whispered as they stretched out on the bed and began undressing each other before fondling, coddling, and exploring.

"I don't think I will need the coffee or brandy, either," Danika whispered. "You are doing a great job of helping me forget my troubles."

"Well maybe we better make this an all-night and maybe tomorrow thing then," Beau grinned.

"Maybe!" Danika conceded.

And that's just what they did! Lying wrapped in his arms made the whole ordeal seem like a faraway dream, and Danika never wanted to wake up from it.

CHAPTER ELEVEN

Danika felt sick all over when she walked into her apartment again. Spending the night with Beau at his place had helped her forget about the terrible tragedy that she had walked into the night before. It had been such a shock when she had opened that apartment door and saw all the damage that she hadn't really been able to think. Now it was all too evident what had happened and what lay ahead for her. She slowly picked enough clothes up off the floor and threw them in an overnight bag, plus grabbed some toiletries, to get her through the next couple of days. The thought of someone strange handling her clean undies made her want to heave. God only knew where their hands had been and what all they had handled before touching her intimate things. She walked to the kitchen and was relieved to find that everything in the refrigerator had been spared and she still had a bottle of Yellow Tail available.

"Do you still want that cup of unfinished coffee?" she asked Beau.

"I'll pass," he smiled. "Do you want me to stick around and take you to wherever you need to go today, or would you rather have a police escort?"

"I can do it on my own," Danika replied. "I don't need an escort. I appreciate all the help you have already given me. Besides, I need you to get to the bottom of all of this."

She didn't want Beau to know that earlier while he had been taking a shower at his place, Ken had called her to let her know that he had heard the news and wanted to meet with her in his office just as soon as possible. Plus, he wanted her to stay with him until everything was settled. She would have to think about that, because staying with Beau had proven to be a pretty nice explosive experience.

But before meeting with Ken, she had to meet with the insurance adjuster. He was coming to the apartment first to look at the damage at ten o'clock and then they would go on to her office. She hoped by then the CSI team would be done with her apartment so she could start cleaning it up. But mostly, she wanted a good hot shower and a good change of clothes, since she was still wearing the ones that she had worn to the Civic Center the night before.

And then she remembered that she had to notify the Iowa Work Force that her employees would be coming in to file for unemployment. She wanted them to have it. They had earned it. It wasn't their fault that some idiot had destroyed their livelihood, as well as hers.

She had called Tara earlier, just as soon as she had crawled out of that snuggly bed of Beau's to tell her the bad news. During the conversation, Danika broke down again and she and Tara had shed some tears together. And as usual, Tara was strong and offered to take the calls from there to make an employee chain, so that Danika didn't have to worry about calling everyone. She had been a very valuable employee for Danika and the thought of not being able to continue working further with her just made Danika queasy inside again.

"I don't want you left alone," Beau was telling her as she shifted her thoughts back to the fact that he was still there with her.

"I'll be fine! I promise! I'll just stay here until the insurance adjuster gets here, and then he will be going with me on to the office to inspect the damage. Besides, CSI will be here doing their thing this morning. I'll be safe. Don't worry!"

Was she trying to convince Beau or herself that she would be safe?

Beau just shook his head. He had already learned that arguing with her was going to get him nowhere.

"Okay," he conceded. "But call me just as soon as you are done with the adjuster, so I can see to it that you have a police escort."

Danika nodded her head in agreement, and gave him a short wave as he left the room, trying not to let him see how she felt inside. She had never been so terrified in her life, and for the first time ever, she didn't feel safe just being on her own. She just wanted to take Beau's handcuffs and attach herself to him. She heaved a big sigh of relief when he opened the door and there stood the CSI unit ready to do their thing. *She wouldn't have to worry about anything as long as they were there with her.*

Danika puttered about the apartment, trying to stay out of the way of progress being made. She had made herself a cup of coffee and offered the working CSI people a cup but they had refused and continued working as if she didn't exist, making her feel just that much more useless. She had already given a sketch artist a description of the man that had been in the hallway the night before when Beau had taken her to the police station to fill out a statement. So now she just had to sit and wait for the insurance adjuster to come, and time was just creeping by. Seconds seemed like minutes, and each minute felt like an hour as she watched the time tick by on her watch.

She was surprised when a man in his late thirties, or maybe early forties, unexpectedly walked into her apartment and extended his hand to her.

"Are you Danika Bronson?" he asked.

Danika stood up and accepted his hand. He was well dressed in a black suit and tie, he had well-groomed dark hair, dark eyes, wore dark rimmed glasses and his smile was to die for.

"Yes! May I help you?"

"I'm here to inspect the damage that you received from the break-in."

"Oh! Well do your thing, and then we can go to my office."

She started to follow him as he began meandering around, looking over the damage, but he said "You don't have to follow me. I can see for myself."

Danika was embarrassed so she receded back to her chair and cup of coffee. He had showed up much earlier than she had expected. Her insurance agent had told her that the adjuster would be there at ten o'clock, and it was just eight fifteen. She watched as he picked up several items including her teddy bear, inspected them, and then put them back where he had found them. A couple of times he and the

CSI people had crossed paths and he was told to leave things alone, which he did, so his time there was short.

"Okay, now we can go to your office," he stated when he returned to the kitchen area where Danika sat watching as much as possible all the activity that was going on inside the four walls of her apartment. There were five members of the CSI unit, and each one was in a different room.

Danika stood up and followed him into the hallway, and when they got to the parking garage below where her car was parked, he said, "Never mind driving. You can ride with me and when we are done, I'll bring you back. Maybe by then the police will be out of here and I can get a better idea of what the damage is."

It made sense to Danika, so she followed him out to the front parking lot to where his silver Audi sat. *Wow! Adjusters must make pretty good money to be dressed as nice as he was and to drive such a fancy car!* He opened the door for her and she slid into a beautiful clean leather interior. The car was loaded with everything that was possible to be in a vehicle.

"Do you know where my office is?" she asked.

"Yes!"

So Danika settled back into her seat and watched out the window when suddenly it hit her. He wasn't taking the usual shortest route to get to her office. In fact, he wasn't even close to going the way he should have been.

"But, you aren't going the right direction to get there."

"That's because I'm not going to your office."

"Why not?"

"I'm not the insurance adjuster."

"If you aren't the adjuster, who are you?"

"Let's just say I'm someone with a job to do and leave it at that," he replied.

"Where are you taking me?" Now panic was swiftly filtering through her whole being.

"Don't ask so many questions."

"I'm not going anywhere with you! Let me out of here!" Danika tried unbuckling her seat belt so she could jump out of the vehicle as it started picking up speed going toward an entrance ramp to the Freeway, heading west out of town. But, the seat belt refused to be released as long as the car was in gear and running.

"Lady, sit down and shut up or I'm going to have to tie you," he warned.

"No!" Danika screamed, as she tried opening the car door. But escaping was not part of his plan. The door wouldn't open because that too, was on auto lock and controlled by the driver of the car. She reached over and tried grabbing his arm, making the car veer and swerve off to the side. Maybe if someone noticed the erratic driving, they would notify the police and they would pull this crazy driver over and then she would be safe.

She didn't see it coming! Her assailant's fist shot out, hitting her square on the end of her nose and cheeks, making her see instant darkness and sending excruciating pain from her nose up into her forehead. How many seconds she was in darkness with only stars surrounding her, she didn't know or try to count. It happened so fast. She just knew that when she was able to see and comprehend everything again, the car was heading south on Interstate #35. She had no idea of the exit number and highway that her assailant pulled off on, but they had only gone west for a couple of miles when he turned south onto a gravel road. The dusty road took them only a short distance into a heavy wooded area before they pulled up to a locked iron gate. Danika quietly watched as her capturer rolled down his window, stuck his hand in front of a camera and the gate opened up. For some reason, the driveway seemed familiar. And then, there it was! She knew instantly where she had seen the driveway before!

The estate was just as beautiful in real life as it had been in the picture. It had to be at least 9000 square feet, not counting the attached four car garage. Just looking at it told her that if it was as fancy on the inside as the outside, it had to be worth at least thirteen to fifteen million dollars. It stood huge with pillars stationed across the front, almost resembling an early plantation home, only different, because she could tell that it had been recently built in the past decade.

Four armed guards dressed in camouflage uniforms stood on the huge balcony of the house, and two stood on both sides of the driveway in front of the home. When the car came to a stop, one of the guards walked to her door and opened it.

"Looks like this little feline gave you some trouble," he laughed as he jerked her out of the car.

"She came easy until she realized I wasn't taking her to her office," the good looking assailant laughed.

"Well, we'll take it from here," the guard grinned and jerked her arm again when she refused to make her feet move to his command. "Move!" he ordered. "Or I'll give you more of the same!"

"Where are you taking me?" Danika bellowed.

"Don't worry about it." He replied in a gruff voice. "It would be a shame to make that pretty face of yours even more swollen than it already is."

Danika could only surmise how her face was beginning to look. She could feel the blood slowly drying that had been trickling from her nose to her lip, and then dripping further down onto her good dress. Her eyes were still watering and burning, and it was getting harder to breathe as her nose began swelling. By the feel of it, she was pretty sure that her nose was broken. That had been the main connecting point of his fist, and it had connected hard. Touching her tender cheeks made her flinch. She could feel them beginning to swell too.

The guard led her up the cement steps into the house, and there she was met by another man whom she quickly recognized. It was the tattooed man that had been in her hallway a couple of nights before.

"You!" she shouted at him as she squirmed, trying to get free of the grasp that was now beginning to hurt. "Why did you destroy my apartment?"

He just started laughing, and took ahold of her already hurting arm, jerking her again to make her walk beside him into a large foyer, down a long hall and into a large room that served as an office for yet another very dark skinned man dressed in an opened bathrobe with spandex swimming trunks underneath. He was fairly good looking, probably in his middle thirties, stood about five feet, seven or eight inches tall, lean and very well built. Large diamond studded earrings adorned both ears, sparkling brighter than his snowy white teeth when he grinned, and his hair was long and thick, braided in tiny rows across his head and strapped into a pony tail at the nap of his neck. He was clean shaven except for a bushy mustache between his nose and mouth. When he spoke, she instantly recognized a Jamaican brogue.

"Welcome to my home, Ms. Bronson. I hope my men have treated you well."

"Do I look like I've been treated well?" she growled.

"I've seen a lot worse," he laughed an evil laugh.

"Why have you had me dragged here?" she implored.

"Obviously you had to be dragged here because you didn't want to come willingly!"

"Obviously! What do you want with me?"

"You have something that belongs to me."

"I can't imagine what on earth I have that belongs to you," she snapped. "If anything, your men or whoever you sent to destroy my apartment have several things of mine."

"Oh that!" he grinned. "If you behave and tell me where you are hiding my diamonds, I might try to see to it that any of your missing items are returned and your apartment restored. However, I can't make any promises."

"What? What are you talking about?" Danika frowned. "I don't know anything about diamonds, let alone any that would belong to you. But you have a diamond ring that belonged to my mother, and I want it back!"

As if she wasn't irritated enough with the man, she became even more irate when he threw his head back and laughed out loud.

"You are in my custody and you think you can tell me what I need to do?" He tapped his chest with his fist and laughed some more. "I like you, Ms. Bronson. Not only are you pretty, but you have spunk. Do you know who I am?"

"Yes, one of my journalists did an article on you and your estate this month! You are Emanuel Vasquez."

"So you *do* know who I am."

"I just don't know why you brought me here! What makes you think you are so great!"

He spread his arms apart. "Look around you. This makes me great!" An evil grin creased his face again.

"You think smuggling drugs into the country and selling them to innocent children and destroying people's lives makes you great? I don't think so!" Danika chided.

"Who said anything about drugs?" he frowned. "I make microchips for the play station!"

"I was told you deal in drugs!"

"Well, you were told wrong. I own a legitimate company that makes games, puts the games on microchips and then sell them to companies that turn them into actual Discs to be played by your *innocent* children and grownups."

"So if you are so damned important, why am I here? I don't have anything to do with your games!"

"I told you! You are here because you have something of mine, and I want them back."

"I know! You said I have your diamonds. But, I don't know what you are talking about." Danika shook her head. "I don't know anything about any diamonds."

"I was told that the man that hijacked my van, killed my driver, and stole my diamonds slipped them in your pocket last Saturday."

"I still don't know what you are talking about. If someone slipped diamonds in my pocket last Saturday, I would have found them when I did my laundry."

"I think you are lying! Why else would you and an FBI agent all of a sudden be playing footsies?"

"How do you know that?"

"I have my way of knowing things, and I know that you are lying about the diamonds. What made you think that as long as you had an agent guarding you, I couldn't get to you?"

"I didn't think that! I mean…, he isn't guarding me because of that!"

Emanuel quickly developed another evil smirk on his face.

"For some reason, I don't believe you. Maybe my men ought to help refresh your memory about what you did with them."

A feeling of despair swept throughout Danika's whole being when she saw the look in his eyes. He reminded her of a wild man that had been touched in the head by some evil force, and she really didn't care about keeping company with him.

Where was Beau Carson now when she needed him?

CHAPTER TWELVE

"Take our guest and lock her in a bedroom. You know which one," Emanuel told the tattooed man that was still holding tight to Danika's arm. "Maybe if she goes a couple of days without food and water, she won't be so cocky and will remember what she did with the diamonds."

Danika tried to no avail to twist free while the tattooed man half drug her up a set of open spiral steps and down a long hall before throwing her on a bed in a large room and locking the door as he left.

"I don't know anything about your damned diamonds!" Danika continued to shout and then ran to the door and started pounding on it with her fists. Finally, when she knew for sure that no one was listening or about to come to her rescue, she stopped the pounding and looked around the room. It was decorated beautifully with modern day furnishings, including the pictures. The furniture in her apartment was expensive, but this was something out of a luxurious dream. The room even held its own bathroom with a Jacuzzi area filled with bottles of imported bath salts, oils, lotions for pampering, and towels and wash clothes that were woven out of Egyptian silk and Indian Ramie, and were unbelievably soft. Awesome! At least she would make good use of that, come bedtime. This room just in itself was something that would make a good story for her magazine; let alone what little she had seen of the rest of the place.

What magazine? She no longer owned a magazine company! And she feared that what she did own had been destroyed beyond repair.

Danika meandered about the room and bathroom, checking out the single window to see if she could possibly get it open to escape out on the balcony. But the window was sealed tight with iron bars on the outside; making her suspect that this room was not used for just any guest that was staying overnight, but for guests like her that was being detained for some special reason or another. The only thing the room lacked for extreme comfort was a television, a bottle of wine, and a phone.

She had no way of trying to get ahold of anyone on the outside. However, while her capturer had been focusing on holding his hand in front of the front gate camera, she had silently slipped her clutch purse with her cellular phone still turned on, under the car seat. Even with her face swelling and hurting, she had enough common sense to know that if Beau or Ken began searching for her, they could ping her phone if it was turned on. And hopefully the car she rode in wouldn't be searched by anyone on the estate.

So she guessed that she would just relax, take a Jacuzzi bath and wait to be found. Surely either Beau or Ken would realize she was missing and start searching for her when she didn't show up at Ken's office or when she didn't give Beau a call to take her home with him. She would show this drug lord that she could go a couple of days without eating. She was used to going without a whole lot of food when she was on assignments. However, living without coffee for a couple of days might be tough. She gritted her teeth and kept telling herself she could do it and maybe…, hopefully…, by the time two days were up, she would be rescued.

But, Danika wasn't the kind to just sit still and do nothing. Ever since she could remember, she had always been active doing something, whether it was working at her place of employment, cleaning house, following Jani with her sports, or keeping busy with her own sports like tennis and golf at one of the clubs in town, or racquetball and swimming at the YMCA. Now, she had absolutely nothing to do. There was no computer to work on, no books or magazines to read, no crossword or word search pamphlets to test her brain with, or television to watch to hear the news. Nothing! She checked out the large walk-in closet only to find it completely empty with only a couple of plastic hangers hanging on the rods. She wasn't an expert, but if they had been wire hangers, she would have tried her luck at undoing the lock from the inside. Darn! The dresser was just as bare as the closet, holding only a pair of satin slippers in one of the drawers. And before long she found herself just pacing from window to the door to listen and then back to the window again. There was nothing to watch outside except the few birds that were flying in and out of the tree tops near her window. It wasn't even noon yet, and she felt herself building up more and more anxiety, and pacing nonstop! Checking her watch every fifteen minutes didn't make the time go any faster, either. If anything, it made the time drag by even slower.

Finally about noon, she decided to take a Jacuzzi bath just to see if that would relax her mind as well as her body. She filled the tub with hot water, added some bath salts and turned the motor and heater on to the tub. Ahhhhh! It felt so good when she climbed in. She slid down into the water enough to cover her breast so that she was completely covered with the foamy, sweet Gardena smelling water. She had just relaxed and shut her eyes when she heard the lock to the door release.

"Stay out!" she yelled, as she tried sliding even further down into the bubbles that were covering her entire body, with the exception of her head, by now.

"Shhhhh! I just brought you a cup of hot broth!" She heard a woman's soft Spanish accented voice. "Please don't let anyone know that I snuck it up here to you. They will hurt me if they find out. I will come back later to get the cup."

And then Danika heard the door close and relock again. And once more she was all alone to think about what her demise was going to be. *What if she couldn't convince them that she didn't have any diamonds or even know what they were talking about?* The soft spoken woman said her own life would be in danger if she was caught bringing anything to Danika. What kind of people would do such a thing?

It was noon and surely Ken or Beau would be wondering by now where she was and soon they should be locating her by the GPS on her phone. She could only hope!

When Danika's skin began looking like a shriveled prune, she shut everything off and climbed out of the tub. She had no alternative but to put her same clothes back on. By that time, the broth had turned cold, but it still tasted good to her. It had been a long time since she had drank a single cup of broth for nourishment. Hopefully, she got to meet the woman that brought it to her so she could thank her properly.

She thought she heard steps coming down the hallway, so she quickly grabbed the empty broth cup and shoved it under the bed, and then sat down on the edge trying to look innocent and contented when the door lock released and her unendowed tattooed man entered.

Danika cringed when he walked across the room and grabbed her by the arm again, jerking her to her feet.

"You could just ask me to come with you! You don't have to be such a son of a bitch!" Danika growled.

"The boss wants to see you again," he grumbled.

"I hope he has better manners than you have, if he expects to get any information out of me!"

With that, the tattooed man threw back his head and laughed a cruel laugh. "Lady, you haven't seen anything yet. And for your own good, I hope you come down off your high horse. I would hate to see them flatten out your nose again."

"You wouldn't dare!" Danika tried squirming her way free from his grasp that was now hurting and burning worse with each twist she tried making to get free.

He dragged her back down the hallway, down the spiral steps again and to a room where Emanuel Vasquez was sitting in an overstuffed leather captain's chair behind a large walnut desk. He had changed clothes since she had seen him, and was now dressed in a pair of white cotton pants with a green and white striped polo shirt.

"I hope you are finding your stay here comfortable." His dark brown eyes glistened, as he let them comb over her from top to bottom. He stood up and walked around the desk to where she stood, his eyes still fixated on her as if he wanted to devour her like one does a turkey leg on the Thanksgiving dinner table. Danika held her breath when he ordered the tattooed man out of the room with a simple wave of the hand. The man nodded and silently left the office, closing the door behind him.

Emanuel walked around her, letting his eyes roam completely over her again.

"You know, you and I could make some beautiful music together," he crooned.

"I don't think so!" Danika snapped. "I'm choosy who I make beautiful music with!"

"I could give you everything you ever wanted and more, if you would just cooperate." He gently ran his fingers down over her cheek. "I guarantee you wouldn't have any more broken noses. You are too pretty to look like you do now. All you have to do is just tell me where you hid my diamonds."

Danika knew how she looked right now, and beautiful she was not! She had glanced at her face each time she walked past the big mirror on the dresser in the room where she was being held captive, and as the day progressed away, her nose was swelling more and starting to turn bluish purple, along with her cheeks and right eye. Not only that, but it was getting harder to breathe.

"I have everything…, I mean; I *had* everything I wanted, and more, until your men came along and destroyed it all."

"And you can have it all back if you want. All you have to do is cooperate."

"And what all does cooperation constitute?"

"Just tell me what I need to know, for starters."

"And, after that?"

"My, my! You are a regular skeptic, aren't you?"

Danika didn't answer. She just looked straight ahead as he continued walking around her, sizing her up.

"My guess is you are about a size eight. Am I right?"

"You aren't answering my question," she replied.

"You could have beautiful dresses, attend royal balls and fly all over the world with me."

"I'm too old for you!" Danika scoffed. "I'm going to be a grandma!"

She couldn't believe those words had just escaped over her tongue and out her lips. It was the first time in the past two days that she had even come close to admitting that she was going to be a grandma, and for some strange reason, the idea of it didn't sound so bad right at the moment, compared to the thought of being locked in this mansion with a snot nosed millionaire that was a drug and diamond dealer and thought she should be more than happy to bow to his wishes and sleep in his bed.

Emanuel let his hand slide from Danika's shoulder to her hand. He picked her hand up and kissed the back of it before his eyes connected with hers. He pursed his lips and said, "Perhaps you need more time to think about it." With that, he clapped his hands together and the office door opened up. Two guards walked in and stood at attention before him.

"Please take our hostage back to her room. She evidently needs more time to think about things."

Before Danika could speak out, the two men had grabbed each of her arms, lifted her off her feet and dragged her back down the hall, up the staircase, and back down the long hall before literally throwing her to the floor in her room. She heard the door being locked once more as she laid there half stunned from the connection with the carpeted floor.

She slowly crawled to the edge of the bed and used it to help pull herself up. Danika wasn't one to cry about things, but for some ungodly reason, she felt like doing it now, and the tears began to slowly trickle down her cheeks. She stretched out across the bed and closed her eyes. Where was Beau or Ken? Why weren't they banging down the door and rescuing her by now?

The afternoon passed and Danika was fit to be tied. There was nothing to do and no one to talk to! Not even the woman who had brought her the broth. Nothing! She curled up on the bed and tried closing her eyes and going to sleep. But that was impossible. One doesn't sleep when there are so many things tumbling through your head. She began pacing again from the window to the door, to the bed, and back to the window again, only to see how the afternoon sun was beginning to drop out of sight. Night was coming and she still hadn't been rescued. Why?

CHAPTER THIRTEEN

Danika switched on one of the lamps that were sitting on the two bedside stands. Finally she slipped out of her dress and pulled the bedspread and sheets back on the bed. The lamp could stay on all night as far as she was concerned. She wasn't about to stay in the dark. Not in this house, anyway. She didn't trust anyone!

She had just glanced at her watch to see what time it was when she heard the lock on her door turn again. She quickly pulled the sheet up to cover her body. Once more it was two guards and trying to hide under the sheets wasn't going to work. And once more, she was jerked to her feet and dragged down the hallway and staircase and forced to stand half naked in front of her abductor.

His eyes combed over her again before he asked, "Are you ready to talk to me?"

"How can I talk to you when I have no idea what you are talking about?"

"I know that the diamonds were placed in your possession."

"I keep telling you that I don't know anything about any diamonds. So if they are in my possession, why didn't you find them?"

"We searched and didn't find them. That's why you need to tell me what you did with them, so I don't have to hurt you."

"What makes you so sure that I have them?"

Emanuel called for his two guards again. "Show this lady what happens when you mess with me and don't talk."

The two guards grabbed ahold of each of Danika's arms and dragged her to a totally different room, and down another set of stairs.

They carried her into a cold, fairly dark room and slammed her into a wooden chair, and before she could utter anything, they were gagging her with a bandana and tying her hands behind the chair. And then they turned on a bright spot light and shot it on another subject that was sitting in the room.

Danika had never been so petrified as when she saw him. It was Marty Vineteri or Andrew Sanchez, or whatever his name was, and he had been beaten almost beyond recognition. His eyes were so swollen and black and blue that she knew it had to be hard for him to even see out of them. He didn't respond when they set her down, and she doubted that he even had enough stamina left in him to know that she was there. One of the guards picked up a bucket of water and poured it over him, and then shook him, trying to revitalize him again so he would talk.

"Do you know this man?" It was Emanuel speaking again. He had followed behind them.

Danika nodded her head.

"Now do you want to talk?"

She shrugged her shoulders.

Emanuel nodded to one of the guards who quickly untied the bandana so she could answer.

"I've only seen him once."

"Where?"

"At the Perkins restaurant in Des Moines."

"Which one?"

Danika told him and when she did, one of the guards left the room.

"I understand he works for your magazine company."

"He contributes articles to my magazine," Danika answered. "A lot of people write and send articles in to us, but I never see them. My publication team deals with them."

Emanuel grabbed Marty's hair and pulled his head back and shouted at him, "Is this the woman that you gave the diamonds to?"

Marty tried squinting at Danika, and then lightly nodded his head.

"No! He's lying!" Danika tried jumping up to her feet, but to no avail, because being tied to the chair wouldn't let her.

"Now, why do you suppose he would lie about that?" Emanuel scowled at Danika. "He knows that he is about to die, so why would he tell me that if it wasn't true?"

"I don't know!" Danika exclaimed. "But I know nothing about any diamonds or him giving them to me."

Emanuel pursed his lips again and said, "And why do you suppose I don't believe you?"

"You've got to believe me!" Danika begged again.

"Nope!" He cast a cruel evil grin at her. "I guess my guards will just have to show you what happens when you lie to me!"

"Don't you touch me! Just as soon as my husband finds me, you'll be sorry!"

"Husband? If you are married, why are you sleeping with an FBI agent?"

"My ex-husband," Danika corrected herself.

Emanuel started laughing, and said, "You are a little bitch, aren't you? And you think you are too good to be my woman? I don't think so!"

Danika didn't answer. She just glared at him.

"So, just how is your ex-husband going to find you way out here?"

"I left my cell phone on and I'm sure by now he is in the process of locating me."

Emanuel tipped his head back and laughed even louder than before. "You mean the cell phone you stuck under the front seat of the car?"

"How did you find it?" Danika was shocked.

"If you weren't such a ditzy bitch, you would have realized that you would be receiving incoming calls and the phone would ring. My driver heard them as he was putting the car in the garage."

Danika's heart sank! "You mean no one knows where I'm at?"

"That's right! Sorry!"

With that, Emanuel left the room and the guard that had left the room came back with a flail. Danika held her breath and then watched as they tied Marty up to a support beam and beat his bare back with it. His screams were deafening, and Danika screamed right along with him with each slap of the whip. When they were through, they left him tied to the post and walked out of the room.

"Oh my God, Marty! Please tell them that I don't have any diamonds," Danika wailed.

"I can't!" she heard him utter slightly above a whisper.

"Why not? You and I both know that I don't have them," Danika pleaded.

"Yes..., you do," he said.

"How?"

"I....stuck them....in....your purse....at the....restaurant," he muttered.

Danika thought about it a second, and then asked, "When?"

"When I.... picked....you up....off.... the floor."

At that, Danika was mortified. If she had the diamonds, where were they? And then she got to thinking about the past few days, and what all they had entailed. The restaurant, her staying with Ken, and then Beau showing up at her office the next day, and it had been a whirlwind ever since then. What purse did she have at the restaurant? And then she remembered. She didn't have her purse. She had been carrying a tote bag with just a few essentials in it, since Ken was supposed to be taking her to Saylorville Dam. So where was the tote bag now? She hadn't touched it since Ken had taken her home and spent the night with her. So if the diamonds were in it, why hadn't they found them when they destroyed everything in her apartment? Somehow, someone had helped themselves to them, and now she and Marty Vineteri were going to be beaten or maybe even killed because of it.

She had no idea why she did, but she suddenly had the idea to start screaming, so she did, and before long, she had the two guards in the room again.

"What's wrong with you, Lady?" One of the men looked at her like he wanted to slap her to shut her up, but the other one actually seemed concerned.

"I want to see your boss again," Danika answered.

"Why?"

"That's for him and me to know. If he wants to know where the diamonds are, he has to come and talk to me."

The guards exchanged glances and then one of them disappeared again, only to return shortly with Emanuel.

"My guard tells me that you are ready to talk." Emanuel was smiling. "I knew you would come to your senses when you saw your partner over there."

"He isn't my partner!" Danika replied. "But, I can tell you where the diamonds went."

"Well, it's about time you came around. Where are they?" Emanuel asked.

"What makes you think I will tell you while I'm tied to this chair in my undies?"

Emanuel nodded and waved to one of the guards to untie her. "Now talk!" he demanded.

"Not until I know what your plans are for me after I tell you where they are!"

"I told you that you and I would make beautiful music together and you would have everything you needed."

Danika frowned. "So are you telling me that I'm going to be stuck here with you instead of being set free?"

"Of course! You certainly can't think that I will set you free so that you can tell the authorities, do you?"

"What's the other alternative?" Danika heard her voice crack as the words passed over her tongue and out her lips.

"You'll be joining your friend, here." Emanuel motioned towards Marty who was now sagging at the knees.

"Send your guards out of the room, and I will tell you," Danika conceded.

"That's my girl! I knew you would start seeing things my way!" Emanuel's eyes lit up like a hungry wolf that had just brought down its prey.

After the guards left the room, Danika asked, "Do you have my laptop?"

Emanuel frowned, and replied, "No! Why? I don't need your laptop."

"Do you have my jewelry box that had my mother's diamond ring in it?"

"No!"

"Well, whoever stole my laptop and jewelry box also has your diamonds."

Emanuel threw his head back and laughed out loud.

"How stupid do you think I am?" he asked. "You'll try anything to get loose, won't you?"

"I'm serious!" Danika scowled. "How well do you trust the men that you sent to search for the diamonds?"

"With my life," he answered.

"Well then, I suggest that you start watching your back, because your life may not be around too much longer," she warned. "I'm telling you that the diamonds were in my tote bag, but they weren't there after your men destroyed my apartment. The diamonds, my laptop, and my jewelry box with my mon's five thousand dollar diamond ring were missing."

Emanuel stood there studying her as if he was weighing every word that she had just said. And then he said, "My men didn't say anything about any of those things. Who else had access to your apartment?"

"No one!"

"So, now you know why I don't believe you, don't you?"

"I swear!" Danika could feel the tears start trickling down her cheeks again, and she couldn't stop them. "Would you at least give me the benefit of the doubt and try to find out?"

Emanuel pursed his lips again as if deep in thought, and said, "I'll give you twenty four hours to tell the truth."

"That goes for Marty, too. It isn't fair for him to be beaten for something he didn't do!"

"Oh, but he did! He stole them in the first place and gave them to you."

Emanuel started for the door, and Danika said, "At least have the decency to untie him and let him sit on his chair."

"I'll think about it," Emanuel answered, and as he reached the door to exit, Danika asked, "Aren't you afraid I will try to escape if you leave me untied?"

"Nope! There isn't any way that you can. I have a guard posted outside your door. Besides, there are security cameras all over the place, so even if you somehow got out, my camera men would spot you and my guards will shoot you on sight." With those words of wisdom, he left the room, and Danika hurried to where Marty still stood tied to the steel support post.

She frantically hurried to untie his wrists, and when she did, he slumped to the floor in a heap. "Come on, Marty! You've got to try to get up."

"Just leave me alone." His whisper was so faint that Danika had trouble hearing him.

"No! Don't give up! We have to believe that someone will find us."

But he refused to help himself get up on the chair and he was too heavy for Danika to pick up by herself. She searched the room for something that she could lay under him as he lay slumped over on the floor. But, she saw nothing! Emanuel had planned this torture room well.

"I have talked to the men who searched your apartment, and they each tell me the same story," Emanuel said as he walked back into the cold dark room again. "They swear that they didn't even see a jewelry box or a laptop."

"And you believe them? Maybe they sold the diamond ring and split the money. You would never know," Danika replied.

Emanuel just shook his head at her. "You'll try anything, won't you?"

And then he walked over and kicked Marty with his foot, rolling him to his back. Marty didn't move, moan, or utter a sound, and Danika's heart sank. Was he just unconscious, or was he dead? And then Emanuel grabbed Danika's chin and squeezed it hard.

"It would be a terrible shame if the same thing was to happen to you."

He dropped her chin and walked back out of the room, leaving Danika more afraid and bewildered than before.

She knelt down and tried feeling Marty's heartbeat. But she couldn't feel anything, so she put her ear to his mouth to see if there was any breath. There was, but it was almost implausible to hear.

Danika shuddered at the thoughts of what all the man had been through before she had even arrived, and what she stood to have done to her if she wasn't rescued quickly, or if she didn't give in to Emanuel's wishes. Which would the lesser of the two evils be? No doubt, going to royal balls and eating with queens or princesses sounded a lot better than being whipped to death. But what if he didn't accept her truth and had her killed anyway? She sat back down on her chair and wrapped her arms her midsection to warm herself up. Suddenly she was freezing cold and the chills had her shivering almost uncontrollably with goose bumps covering her entire body. She stood up and began pounding on the door again.

"What do you want, now?" The guard grumbled when he opened the door.

"Get me some clothes or a blanket, because I'm freezing."

"Get used to it!" he growled.

"You either get me something to keep me warm or I will beat on this damned door all night!"

The guard frowned at her and replied, "I'll ask the boss and see what he says."

"Make it quick!" Danika shouted as he closed the door.

There was only one small window at the top of the room, so Danika pulled the chair over to the wall and climbed up, hoping to catch a glimpse of the outside. Thank God, there was still a bit of daylight outside. But, she knew sunset and then darkness wasn't very far off. And that meant she would be left alone in this cold, dark, desperate room all night. And that in itself made her feel like she was about to go off the deep end. She couldn't stand to be in a totally dark room. Ever since she was a little tike she needed a night light to sleep by. *Where was that guard and what was taking him so long?*

From the window Danika could see the lights that were shining on the front gate of the property, and there were two guards in front of it that were constantly pacing back and forth, as if they were in the military, and as near as she could remember, there was only one lane that led to that gate, so if anybody was coming to rescue her, they would be seen before they even got near it. Darn!

The thought of her cell phone being destroyed didn't make her feel any better, either. Her not-so-brilliant idea had just made things worse for her, instead of better. Darn that driver! Why hadn't he hurried up and gotten out of the car before the phone rang? But more so, what had she done to deserve all this? She had always paid her taxes and gave to UNICEF, and hadn't she always donated to the Save the Trumpet Swan's foundation every year? Maybe this was God's way of punishing her for being promiscuous. That's what she got for sleeping with two different men in the same week. Or was this her punishment for not wanting to be a grandma?

"Please dear God, I promise I won't go to bed with another man again unless I'm married to one, and I will try real hard to be a good grandma, even if I don't want to be one, if you will just get me out of this mess," she prayed out loud, and then added, "Plus, I will start giving more money to the Lonely Puppy Rescue League." Then she moved her chair back to where it had previously been in hopes the guard didn't open the door and catch her before she got there.

She had just sat down when the door opened again and the guard entered carrying a blanket. He threw it at her and said, "There! The boss okayed it so I had to go find one for you."

It was a heavy woolen green blanket that they issue to men and women in the military, and even though it felt awesome to her now chilled through body, it smelled horrible. One whiff and she hated to think of all the places that blanket had been or what all it had been through. But, she wasn't about to complain about it, for fear the guard would take it away from her, and that, she didn't want. She didn't care if it did smell and made her itch, she was going to wrap herself up in it and be thankful there weren't any rats in this God forsaken dungeon of a room.

Danika tried dozing while sitting upright in her chair, and quickly found that wasn't going to work. And as the night settled in, and the darkness filled the room, she liked being where she was even less. Plus the thought of being in the same dark room with a near to close death person made the fears just grow. Was she ever going to be rescued, or was she doomed to die just like Marty Vineteri was? She had never been a quitter, but for some ungodly reason, she was feeling like being one now. She just wanted to curl up in the corner and cry herself to death. That is, if she was really destined to die. She didn't want to experience the pain that Marty had been through. Just the thought of it made her shudder with more chills. Was she really cold, or was it just fear of the unknown?

Danika had never put through such a long fearful night in her entire life. Her only salvation was the outside lights that circled the large driveway, shining through the small window. She spent most of the night standing on the chair in front of the window, just to help keep her sanity.

She couldn't tell if Marty was still breathing or not, but she hadn't heard him move or utter any sounds, since it had gotten dark. He had moaned a couple of times before it got dark, but now she heard nothing except the constant gurgling coming from her stomach. A day without anything to eat except a bagel and a cup of broth was beginning to take its toll on her. Not only did she feel half nauseous from hunger, but her head was beginning to hurt from lack of caffeine. She thrived on caffeine by drinking at least eight to ten cups of coffee a day, especially when she was trying to meet deadlines. Tara had always made sure that there was a fresh pot of coffee brewing for her.

If she could just keep her sanity through the night, she was thinking of selling her soul to the devil in the morning and giving in to Emanuel just so she could maybe get a cup of coffee and hopefully wouldn't have to go through any severe torture before being beaten to death.

Danika was just stepping down off the chair when a flash caught the corner of her eye. Or was it a flash? She quickly stepped back up on the chair and searched as far as she could see, trying to locate where the flash came from. But, she saw nothing! She waited and waited, but nothing caught her eye again, so she guessed she had just been seeing things. Or maybe she was just hallucinating from starvation and paranoia.

And then she saw it again, and she swore it had come from up in the trees! It was just one single flash. But it had happened so fast, that she wasn't sure if she had actually seen something or if she was just hoping she had seen something. And then once again, there was nothing. Disheartened and discouraged, she stepped down off of the chair and sat on it, just to rest for a while. It wouldn't do any good to shut her eyes, because she knew she wouldn't get any sleep even if she tried. And she wasn't about to lie on the cold damp cement floor.

Then all of a sudden she could have sworn that she was hearing gun shots. But, they were so faint that once again she felt like she was only dreaming of sounds that she wanted to hear, and not the actual thing. She stepped back up on the chair and peered out the window towards the front gate, and was surprised that she couldn't see the two guards that had been standing there previously.

But then she saw boots running past her window, and those flashes were coming now from several different directions out of the darkness. What was going on?

She was still standing on the chair trying to see what was happening outside, when the door to the room flew open and the guard hurried in. Before she could ask any questions, he had grabbed her arm and was bending it around behind her.

"Ouch! What are you doing?" she yelled, as he started pushing her toward the door, and continued out into the hallway.

"The boss wants you!" he snarled. "And don't give me any crap or I will drop you right here!"

Danika could see by the look on his face, that he meant business, so with adrenaline pounding through her veins, she stumbled ahead of him as he pushed her up the steps and to the office where Emanuel was standing. The look on Emanuel's face was just as cold and evil as the guards. He instantly grabbed her arm from the guard and pushed her over to a window.

He cranked it open and yelled, "Leave now, if you want her alive."

"We can't do that!" a voice out of the darkness yelled back. "Tell your men to throw down their weapons and all of you come out. We have you surrounded."

Emanuel hurriedly cranked the window shut again and threw Danika down in one of the large overstuffed chairs in the room. And then he mumbled, "Damn Feds, anyway. They'll find out they can't order me around and get by with it."

Danika tried to jump up off of the chair, but he pushed her down again, and screamed at her to sit down and be quiet, while he figured out what he was going to do.

He started pacing the floor and one of the guards came hurrying into the room to give him an account of the ones that had already been brought down outside. Emanuel jerked Danika up to her feet again and once more pushed her to the window. Once more he cranked it open and shouted, "I'm going to my car and I'm coming through. And if you don't want her shot, then I suggest you hold your fire and let us pass." Then Emanuel yelled at the guard to get his driver so he could leave.

"But he was shot as he went charging outside when the shooting started," the guard objected.

"Where's your precious body guard that robbed my apartment?" Danika smirked. "Where are all of your tough guys now?"

Little was she prepared for the fist that hit her in the nose and mouth, sending her whole head spinning with instant pain. And from the tingling feeling that followed, she knew her nose was dripping blood, and she had no way to stop it.

Once more, Emanuel jerked her to her feet. "You know how to drive, smart mouth! You are going to get us out of here."

"Can't you do your own damned driving?" she asked as he started pushing her out of the office and down the hall.

"I can! But why should I put myself in the front seat? If they start shooting, it will be you they hit, and not me."

"Could I at least have some decent clothes on?" she demanded.

"No! We haven't got time!"

He continued to push her to the garage, with the guard leading the way. When they reached the garage, the guard scoped it out first to make sure it was safe for them, and then he opened the car door for Emanuel to climb in the back seat. As he shoved Danika in the front seat, Emanuel stated, "This car has bullet proof windows in the back seat, so I won't be the one that gets shot. We'll see how your sleeping buddy likes that!" And with that, an evil laugh escaped his throat.

He handed Danika the keys as the guard climbed in beside her. Emanuel was making sure that he was going to be the only one that escaped the wrath of the federal agents and troopers that were outside in the darkness. Danika was sure that it was Beau's voice that she had heard. Or, maybe it was just wishful thinking. It didn't matter! If they tried to shoot, she would be shot by her own savior.

Not only did Emanuel make sure that she knew how to start the car, but after she did, he closed the bullet proof window between the front and back seats.

The Coward!

Danika slowly backed the car out of the garage. All was quiet! But then she put it in forward gear and stepped as hard as she could on the gas pedal to make it surge out of the circular driveway.

"What are you doing?" the guard yelled.

Danika didn't answer. She just applied all of her strength on the foot feed.

"Stop and push the button to open the gate!" the guard yelled again while trying to reach the remote that controlled the gate. "We're going to crash!"

But he yelled too late, because when they reached the gate, she didn't wait for it to open. Instead, she sent the car crashing through the heavy wrought iron bars, plummeting on into the trees and thickets that surrounded the lane.

All she remembered was the scraping noise of the car as it crashed through the Iron Gate and the shattering of the glass, before the air bags deflated, smacking her in the face and knocking her out.

CHAPTER FOURTEEN

Danika woke up to all kinds of red, white and blue flashing lights surrounding her, plus too many bustling bodies to count, and she was being gently pulled out of the car that now had a nose on it looking like an accordion. But even as gently as she was being moved, she was feeling pain from every possible nerve and muscle in her body, mainly in her neck and back.

"Danika! Can you hear me?" It *was* Beau's voice that she had heard, and right now the sound of it was like hearing a favorite song on the radio. She wanted to hear it again and again just to be sure she wasn't dreaming. Or, to be sure she hadn't died and was now reincarnated. She was sure she was alive, and if she hadn't been in the process of being strapped to a gurney, she would have pinched herself just to make sure of it.

She didn't see Beau at first since she was surrounded by EMTs that were putting a neck brace on her and trying to slide a flat board in under her as soon as they pulled her from the car. But there he was, taking a hold of her hand and squeezing it, before the Paramedics shoved her on into an ambulance and closed the door. But, not before she had a chance to see that there were at least five or six men and women in uniform surrounding the car with guns pointed, ordering Emanuel out of the back seat. She didn't see the guard, so she assumed that he had either been pulled out of the car and had been arrested already, or maybe still passed out with his face buried in the deflated airbag.

The trip to the hospital emergency room was a busy one, with EMT's yelling at her to keep her awake, plus trying to keep her face covered with an oxygen mask. As soon as she entered the hospital she was whisked to a curtained room where nurses and doctors were swarming around her asking all kinds of questions which she couldn't answer with the mask over her nose and mouth, and poking her stomach and ribs to see if they thought she had any broken ribs.

"Did she know her name? Did she have pain anywhere? And if so, where?"

All she could do was try to either nod or shake her head to answer any questions they were throwing at her.

"Can you lift your left arm?" one of the medical team was asking. Since Danika still couldn't talk, she lifted her left arm to show them. It was then that she saw the blood running down to her elbow from a jagged cut in her forearm. Probably from the glass that she heard shattering.

"Can you lift your right arm, Ms. Bronson?" Danika was able to lift her right arm, but it was hurting in the shoulder when she did so. However, it was blood free, so that was a good sign.

"Now lift your left leg up off of the table."

Danika did as she was told. Or so she thought.

"Ms. Bronson, please lift your left leg up off the table."

She shoved the mask to the side of her face and said, "I am!"

"Can you lift your right leg up for us?"

"Yes!" she answered. But then she saw the concerned look on the whole medical team's faces as they talked.

"Are your legs cold?" one of them asked.

*Of course her feet and legs were cold! That was a dumb question. She had been stuck in that dark cold room with no clothes for at least eight hours. How could she **not** be cold?*

"Can you feel this?" the younger, good looking doctor asked.

She felt nothing, and since her head was being held tight in the neck brace, she couldn't tip it up to see what she was supposed to be feeling.

Again the doctor asked, "Can you feel this?" And once more, she felt nothing but the cold and numbness.

And then she saw and realized that they had been touching her feet and legs with a needle, and she wasn't feeling the sting. It was just the numbness and cold shooting from her toes to her hip!

She watched as the medical team started discussing things in a low tone so she couldn't hear, and it irritated her to no end.

"If you are going to talk about me, at least have the decency to talk out loud so I can hear you!" she bristled. "I'm a big girl! I can take anything you have to say about me."

"We are concerned that you aren't feeling us touch your legs and feet, so I'm sending you to have some x-rays taken before we do any diagnosing. Okay?" The good looking doctor told her.

"Do you have any relatives or anyone that we need to be contacting for you?" a sweet oriental nurse asked.

"Why? Am I about to die?" fear gripped Danika's whole being. Had she escaped the wrath of Emanuel and his brutes just to be killed by the heathen's car?

"Not if we can help it!" the young doctor laughed. "But just in case you surprise us and do something foolish that we aren't expecting, we need to be prepared. Also, we always try to work with the police when people are brought in to us like this."

"Okay," Danika smiled. "Please contact Kenneth Bronson at the DA's office. If any decisions are to be made, he can help me make them."

"How is he related to you?"

"He's my ex-husband and still a good friend. He can contact our daughter that lives in Colorado."

Jani! How would she deal with any of this? Danika guessed she would just have to wait to see what the diagnosis was, before she started worrying. But down deep in her stomach, she could feel the bees buzzing. Why couldn't she lift her legs and why couldn't she feel anything?

The medical team separated and two nurses pulled her bed out of the curtained room and hurried her down another hall to a small room with a large x-ray machine. First she was transferred from the bed over onto a table, still strapped to the flat board that the EMT's had slid under her at the wreck.

"Don't breathe!" one of them said, so even as bad as it hurt to hold her breath, Danika did as she was told. Then they moved her to each side, still strapped, and still holding her breath when she was told to do so. She started feeling a sickening nausea creep into her whole being.

"I think I'm going to be sick," she whispered. And she knew that if she had any food in her stomach at all, heaving is just what she would do and there wouldn't be any way of stopping it.

"We'll be done soon," one of the nurses sympathized with her. "But we have one more test to do."

They transferred her to another room that was a bit larger than the one before, slid her onto another cold table and strapped her down even more so she couldn't move a muscle even if she wanted to. And then they slowly pushed her into a huge cylinder with a red light that just kept circling back and forth over her entire body, from top to bottom. Then as they pulled her out, one said, "Now lift your knees and hold them in a bent position." Danika tried and tried to do so, but the knees refused to bend.

"What's wrong? Why won't they bend?" Danika implored.

"That's what we are trying to find out," one of them answered.

Both nurses lifted the knees to the bending position that they needed by sticking pillows in under them and did the whole thing in the cylinder all over again.

The horrible realization that there had to be something terribly wrong was finally hitting Danika, and she didn't know how to accept it. The reality of what all could be wrong was starting to filter through her brain. Had she severed a nerve in her back? Would she ever be able to walk?

She was glad when the two nurses were finally finished with her and wheeled her back to the warmth of the emergency room stall that she had been in. They had no sooner reached the small confinement when Danika's teeth started chattering. She was cold, and she was hungry.

"Damn!" Danika swore when both nurses disappeared out of the room. "I'm laying here in my undies, fully exposed to whoever sticks their damn nose in here, plus starving and freezing to death, and they walk out and just leave me!"

She was searching as best that she could with her arms still strapped down, to find the call light. Even though she saw it, she couldn't reach it! She was just opening her mouth to scream as loud as she could to get some attention, when one of the nurses returned with three hot, cotton flannel blankets and spread them out over Danika's entire body. Sheer luxury! She hadn't felt this warm since she had climbed out of the hot tub in the bedroom that she had been locked in earlier. And then she began to wonder just how long it had been since she had been abducted? There had been no way to know by being locked in a dark, dreary, cold room before she had been dragged to the garage and shoved into the car.

"What time is it?" Danika asked when the nurse stepped back into the little room with all the makings of sticking an intravenous needle in the back of her hand.

"It is just past five AM."

"Is it possible for me to have some coffee or some broth?" Danika asked. "I haven't had anything to eat since yesterday morning."

"I'm sorry," the nurse replied much to Danika's regret. "Until we know if you have any internal injuries, we are supposed to withhold all food and liquids. That's why I'm about to start feeding you through a couple of tubes."

Danika swore she was being just as tortured in the hospital as she had been in Emanuel's custody. She swore even louder when the nurse stuck that needle in the side of her wrist and started taping it down. And being strapped down to this gurney and not being able to move wasn't helping her attitude any. After the nurse left the cubicle, Danika suddenly had the urge to just start crying, and it made her angry at not only herself, but everybody and everything around her, since crying wasn't her style. To make things worse, she couldn't even use her hands to wipe the tears away, so they just streamed down her cheeks and onto the pillow.

All kinds of woes and worries kept swarming through her head. Was she going to be disabled due to all of this, and if so, how would she survive? Emanuel would be going to jail if she was at all able to testify at his trial. His trial? Would she even be able to press charges on him? Was Marty Vineteri still alive? If he survived, was he in one of these little curtained off rooms being treated like she was? Why wasn't someone coming back in to talk to her? Surely by now they knew what the x-rays showed. What was taking them so long? Ticking minutes seemed like exasperating hours, and it was driving her crazy. Patience was not one of her virtues and dwelling on the past twenty four hours was taking its toll on her mind and soul.

And then it slowly all became like a bad dream as she unknowingly slipped off into la-la land.

CHAPTER FIFTEEN

"Sweetheart! I came just as soon as I heard. Are you okay?"

Danika tried opening her droopy eyes to the vehement tone of a man's voice. "I...I don't know ...," she tried answering. She hadn't been called sweetheart for an eternity, or so it seemed. So who was calling her that now? Somehow, she managed to get her eyes focused on the figure standing over her. And the minute she saw Ken and the concerned look on his face, she began wailing full force. For some ungodly reason, she just wanted to unload all of her woes on to someone, and he just happened to be the first one to appear so she could do so. She couldn't blink enough to keep the tears from flooding over the dam and down her cheeks as she poured out her heart and soul to him between the wailing.

Ken tried gathering her into his arms as best he could with her still strapped to the table. "There, there! Don't cry, Honey. Everything is going to be okay," he soothed.

"But it's not okay!" Danika cried. "Oh Ken, it has been a terrible nightmare! First my apartment and office were destroyed, and then I was kidnapped by a guy who said he was the insurance adjuster, and then I saw Marty being beaten to death, and now I don't have any feeling in my legs."

"What are you talking about?" Ken frowned. "Who kidnapped you?"

"Emanuel Vasquez and his army of inhumane men," Danika continued to wail. They dragged me down a long hall and then locked me into a room without any coffee, and then dragged me down some more steps and locked me in a cold dark room without any clothes!

"You were naked?"

"No..! I had my undies on. But that was all!"

"Did they rape you?"

"No. But I was afraid that SOB was going too when he wouldn't leave his hands off of me!"

"Who?"

"Emanuel! He told me that if I would confess to where I put the diamonds, he would treat me like royalty."

"What diamonds?"

"I don't know! He thinks I have his diamonds, but I don't even know what he was talking about. That's why they tore up my apartment. They were looking for diamonds, plus someone stole the jewelry box that you gave me that had my mom's diamond ring in it."

"What made them think you had stolen diamonds?"

"Before he died, Marty Vineteri told me he had put them in my purse at the restaurant the other day when he bumped into me."

"Marty is dead?"

"I don't know. I couldn't hear him breathing in the dark."

Ken frowned as if he wasn't quite sure what she was talking about, or if he even believed her.

"Honest!" Danika continued to cry.

Ken reached in his pocket, pulled out an initialed white handkerchief, and wiped the tears off of her cheek as best he could, considering they were flowing nonstop.

"That's why I told you to be careful after I saw the picture and article for your magazine. I was afraid something like this might happen," he admonished her as if he was scolding a small child.

Danika didn't answer. She didn't want to admit that maybe he was right for once, and that she should have listened.

"But how did they get into my apartment and office?"

"Criminal minds will always find a way," Ken replied. "Since your magazine is all about living in a fairy tale world, you have no idea of what the real world is really like.

After a few seconds of silence, Ken asked, "Is that why you didn't show up at my office yesterday?"

"Yes! Weren't you concerned about it?"

"Yes and no!" he grinned. "I know how set in your ways and stubborn you can be."

"Did you try calling me?"

"Yes, but it went into voicemail right away, and then I had to be in the court room by noon, so I didn't try anymore."

"And after court?"

"What do you mean?"

"What did you do after court?"

Ken's face turned a slight shade of red. "Lauren and I worked late on a case back at the office."

Danika tried to smile, but the fact that she knew what they were doing back at the office hurt just as bad as the day he had admitted that he was having sex with Sonya. The man was never going to change!

"It's probably a good thing that you weren't stuck with me staying with you. Wasn't it?"

"What makes you say that?" Ken asked.

"Have you talked to Jani yet?" Danika changed the subject.

"No! I came here just as soon as I was notified that you were in a car accident. Nobody said anything about you being kidnapped!"

"Who notified you?"

"A couple of policemen came knocking on my door about six o'clock this morning."

"I'm sorry that they bothered you," Danika stated. "They asked me who they should notify and the only one I could think of was you. I thought you should let Jani know."

"How did your car accident happen?"

Danika tried turning her head away in hopes the tears would stop their endless running. But once again, the neck brace kept her from doing so.

"I was trying to escape!" she finally stated, as the curtain to the cubical was quickly drawn back.

"Ms. Bronson, I have some good news and some bad news for you," the young good looking doctor said as he stepped inside the corridor of the small confinement. And then he stuck his hand out to Ken and said, "I'm Dr. Sheppard. Are you her husband?"

"Well, yes and no," Ken grinned. "I'm her ex-husband for the time being."

Dr. Sheppard scowled and nodded as if wondering just what Ken meant.

"Just tell me what the good news, bad news is," Danika quipped.

"What do you want to hear first?" Dr. Sheppard asked.

"Give me the bad news first," Danika answered.

"Well! The bad news is that you have a couple of fractured vertebrae in your back. They aren't broken, so that is good news. Plus, the accident caused you to have severe whiplash. Thank goodness, you had your seatbelt on, and the vehicle you were in obviously had a good air bag system, or else you would probably have a lot more damage to some bones and ribs to go with it."

"Why do I hurt so bad if that's all that's wrong?"

"Tell me again where you hurt," Dr. Sheppard told her.

Danika explained, and he replied, "I'm sure you have a lot of bruising that's causing the pain."

"So why can't I feel anything in my back and legs, if that's the bad news?"

"I'm going to send you down for an MRI to make sure none of the nerves in your spine were severed or damaged. We won't know for sure what to expect until those results come back."

"If that's the bad news, what's the good news?" Danika asked.

"The good news is that if there aren't any damaged nerves, you can expect to get the feeling back in your legs as soon as the swelling goes down."

"How long will that take?" Danika felt like she wanted to barf. The thought of having to spend the rest of her life in a wheel chair did not sound very appealing to her.

"Maybe a week! Maybe a month! I can't answer that," Dr. Sheppard scowled. "In any event, you can plan on staying here with us for at least ten days or longer, depending on how quick those vertebras mend and how you respond to physical therapy."

"Do I have to stay strapped down like this?" Danika could feel the rush of tears start running down her cheeks again.

"Not if you behave!" Dr. Sheppard smiled. "I'll tell the nurse to unstrap your arms so you can use the call light. Just as soon as the MRI is done, and we can find an empty room, you can have a little more comfort and privacy. In the meantime, relax and enjoy your stay."

"Can I please have a cup of coffee?" Danika asked as he slid the curtain back to exit. "I've got an awful headache and I know it's from lack of caffeine."

"Part of your headache could be caused by the whiplash. But, as soon as they get you settled in your own room, you can have something to eat and drink. In the meantime, you'll just have to try to tolerate it until we are done running tests. You are getting Demerol for pain right now, so that should help."

With that, he was gone, and Danika didn't know if she should feel relieved or upset with the news he had just delivered to her. Never in her life had she been on such a rollercoaster ride of emotions. She thought she had been through it all after the divorce, and then being kidnapped. But those setbacks had been nothing like what she was facing now. She knew if she looked Ken in the face right now that she would be a basket case. Yet, she was glad that he was there with her to hear the news. Now it was up to him to tell Jani. And how would she accept hearing the fact that her mother might be confined to a wheel chair the rest of her life and wouldn't be able to provide for her like Danika had done all throughout Jani's life. Even though Jani had chosen to live with her Dad, it had been her mother's wealth that had provided for her every wish and whim that she had wanted. Now Danika's future looked pretty dim. How could she rebuild her company, provide for her mother's nursing home care, and help Jani if she was restricted to a wheel chair? Who was going to take care of her?

"There's no sense of you calling Jani until we have the final results back," Danika sniffled as Ken stepped back by her bedside.

"Is there anyone else you want me to call?" he asked.

"I would tell you to call the girls and Tara, if I had their telephone numbers. But I have no idea what Emanuel's thugs did with my phone. And," she heaved a big sigh, "since my laptop was stolen the night my apartment was broken into, I don't have access to any addresses or phone numbers that were recorded on it."

"Your laptop was stolen too?" Ken frowned.

"Yes!" Danika scowled. "You sound surprised. Why?"

Ken just shook his head.

"Emanuel swore that his men didn't steal my laptop or my jewelry box. But, I don't believe him. He said they didn't have any use for it. I just think they didn't want him to know that they had the diamond ring."

"Probably," Ken agreed. "A thief is a thief and it doesn't make any difference who they steal from. They'll even steal from their mama and best friend."

"Well, I guess it doesn't make any difference now. What's done is done."

"I still belong to the same country club as Bruce Humphry, so I'm pretty sure that I can get ahold of Alma for you. She should be able to let the other girls know that you are in here to stay for a while," Ken said with a smile on his face.

"That would be great!" Danika answered. But then she wondered if she really wanted to see anyone until she knew. Because if she was going to spend the rest of her life in a wheel chair instead of doing workouts at the Y or playing golf with the girls, she wasn't sure she wanted anyone to know just yet, and she knew the girls would want to know every little detail of what all she had been through and what she was going to do next. She wasn't used to being doted on, and she definitely didn't want it now. She just wanted to be left alone until she knew what to expect.

About that time a nurse came in and unstrapped Danika's free arm and hand and handed her the call light, and then checked both bags hanging over Danika's head that were feeding liquids into her veins. When she was done, she looked at Ken and said, "We are going to wheel her down for a MRI, so If you want, you can wait for her in the waiting room. We will come and get you when we get back."

"How long will that take?" Ken asked.

"She will be gone at least forty five minutes or longer. They have to work her in with their scheduled appointments. And then hopefully, there will be a room ready for her when she is done, but we won't know for sure until then."

"Maybe I need to leave and take care of business, and then come back later. Will that work?" Ken asked Danika as he squeezed her hand.

"By then, we should know what to tell Jani," Danika tried smiling. Even as much as she tried her best to sound cheerful, she had all she could do to hold the tears back as she watched the curtain fall between her and Ken when he exited the small room. How could anyone love and hate a person at the same time? She didn't know, but that was what she was feeling right now towards the man. Part of her heart wanted to restore the love that she had always felt for him and part of her hated him for forcing his way back into her life and stirring up old heartaches.

Before long, she was whisked onto another cold gurney and wheeled into an elevator, down a long hall and into another freezing room. She swore this had to be the coldest hospital she had ever been in. What was up with that? Thank goodness she still had a light weight cotton flannel sheet over her. It wasn't warming her up, but it was at least covering her up so that she wasn't completely exposed to the ice cold room and surrounding elements. Her teeth were chattering so, that she could barely comprehend all the instructions the technicians were giving her as they prepared her to have the MRI.

"We are going to be injecting a dye into your veins, but you won't feel it because we are going to use the port that has already been installed."

"That's g-g-g-o-o-d!" Danika whispered. "I've been through e-e-enough h-h-hell for one d-d-day."

The technician laughed and said, "I'm afraid you aren't done yet."

"What d-do you m-mean?"

"When I tell you too, I want you to put your arms over your head and reach as far as you can reach. And then hold it like that and don't move while the Images are being taken."

"Y-y-you've g-got to b-be k-k-kidding me!"

"No! I'm afraid not!" he smiled. "The best thing you can do while you are in the machine is close your eyes, relax, and just try to think of good thoughts. Maybe even try to go to sleep."

"Go to sleep?" Danika didn't chatter. "How damn long am I going to be in that thing?"

"As long as it takes to get all the images that we need of your spinal column. Maybe fifteen, twenty minutes or so!"

"Oh my God! Can't you knock me out or something? I hate close confinements."

"You are already on Demerol and Valium, so no, we can't give you anything more. You just need to try relaxing."

"Where's my Yellow Tail when I need it?" Danika wailed.

"Your what?" the technician scowled.

"My Yellow Tail wine!" Danika almost yelled.

She knew by the look he gave her that he was thinking the same thing that she had been hearing from Ken all the past week. Heaven forbid! *Maybe she had become a wino and* needed *to attend those AAA meetings?* But right now she wasn't going to worry about it. The two technicians were wheeling her up to and into the imaging canister. *Dear God help me!*

Danika's room was waiting for her following the MRI and with it came a fresh cup of coffee. She had never appreciated a good swallow of coffee so much in her entire life. The coffee and the warm blankets they were piling on her felt like Heaven and she snuggled down in under them to absorb the luxury of it all.

Contrary to what she thought about the MRI, she survived the whole twenty minutes of the pure torture of not being able to move or pull her arms to her side. Not only did she feel numb when they pulled her out of the canister but her brain refused to function properly for a few minutes. Instead of concentrating on what was taking place, she had relived the whole terrible nightmare of being placed in the cold dark room with a half dead person back at Emanuel's estate. How could a person relax or go to sleep with such an abhorrent thing running through their mind? How many nights would she wake up in the future reliving the whole scenario over again?

"You're a hard person to find!"

Danika opened her eyes to the sound of a most welcome voice. There stood Beau in the doorway of her room holding a couple of red and pink heart shaped *Get Well* helium balloons, plus a dozen long stemmed yellow roses in a crystal vase.

For as long as she could remember, she had never been this happy to see someone. And when that handsome face smiled at her she appreciated seeing him all the more. Even though he had on his war torn work suit, he was dressed like a king as far as she was concerned. But, yellow roses instead of red? Evidently the night they spent together didn't mean as much to him as it did her. They meant that she was a friend instead of a lover. She fought hard to hide her disappointment as he walked on into the room and sat the roses on a shelf on the wall.

"How are you feeling?" he asked as he turned and walked closer to her bedside.

"Like I've been ran over by a semi," Danika grinned.

"I'm so sorry," he half whispered. "I should have stayed with you and never left you alone."

"If I remember right, I sent you out the door," Danika replied.

"Yes, but I should have known better than to let you persuade me like that." He reached out and took ahold of her hand that she now had lying on top of the blankets. "I don't usually let pretty women talk me into doing things I don't want to do."

"Oh, so now it's my fault?" Danika teased. "I suppose letting me sleep in your bed was my fault too?"

"No!"

She could see the red creep up his neck and into the five o'clock stubble that was covering his face.

"About that...I'm sorry that I let it happen. Believe me when I say I've never slept with any of the victims that I've ever given shelter to before."

Did she apologize, accept his apology, or brush it off as a mistake that they both made and let it go at that? It wasn't going to matter which option she took, it hurt to know that now he thought it was a mistake. And why she was feeling hurt by it, she couldn't determine right now. She had never felt like this about anyone except Ken. So what was it about this man?

"Well, just chalk it up to helping a mixed up girl get what she needed for the night and let it go at that," she smiled.

"No hard feelings?" he asked.

Danika shook her head. *What did he expect out of her? She wasn't just another chick that he picked up off the street. She actually had feelings like any respectable girl would have.*

"No hard feelings," she stated.

"As soon as you feel like it, I need a statement from you concerning your kidnapping."

"Maybe tomorrow! Right now, I just need to get some rest and give my mind time to clear," Danika answered.

"Sure! I understand," he winked. "From the looks of it, you've been through a lot. Did they beat you or did your face get bruised from the accident?"

"Both!"

"Okay!" He squeezed her hand again. "I'm glad you are alive and able to talk. That's more than Mr. Vineteri or Sanchez or whatever the hell his name is, can do."

"Did.., did he live through it?"

"No. So now we will never know for sure what all he was involved in."

"Maybe my statement tomorrow will help."

"Great! I will see you sometime tomorrow, then." He let go of her hand and turned and walked out of her room leaving Danika feeling just about as empty inside as she had ever felt.

Danika slept as much as possible in between the times that the nurses were coming in and checking her blood pressure, squeezing her hands, sticking her feet with needles, and checking the clear liquid bags of what they called her food feeding into her veins. The only coffee she had gotten to consume was that one heavenly cup that helped warm her up. She was not able to feel the needles being stuck into her feet, and that had her upset. When would she find out for sure what to expect? Would she or would she not ever be able to walk again?

It was late afternoon when Ken walked into her room again. In his hand he was carrying her favorite bouquet of summer flowers consisting of daisies, sunflowers and carnations. His smile faded when he saw the yellow roses sitting on the shelf and the balloons that were tied to her bed.

"Were the girls here?" he asked.

"No! Not that I know of," Danika replied.

"So who brought you the flowers?"

"Why? Does it matter to you?" she cast him a wry smile.

"Of course! I would like to think that I still account for something in your life."

"You do! You are my daughter's father. That accounts for something," Danika teased. "Without you, I wouldn't have her."

Ken frowned and moved the yellow roses over so that there was room for his bouquet to sit on the shelf too.

"Have they told you anything yet?" he asked as he sat down in the recliner sitting next to her bed.

Danika shook her head. "The technicians that did the MRI said it might take a couple of days before they would know for sure."

"I got ahold of Jani, and she said that she would try to catch a flight out tonight."

"It will seem so good to see her again," Danika smiled.

"Yes!" Ken agreed. "I told her that I would reimburse her the money for the ticket. It sounds like they might be a little bit strapped right now."

Danika thought about it a second and asked, "Then why did they decide to get pregnant now?"

"I'm not sure. I just know that if we would have waited for the most appropriate time and for our pocketbooks to be full, we never would have had her. We survived it!"

Danika knew he was right. The main part of her wealth came after the divorce, and after her company began to grow. And she wasn't sure how Ken stood now.

"Did you get ahold of Alma?" she changed the subject.

Ken started laughing. "No, not yet! I haven't been to the country club yet."

"I'm sorry," Danika laughed, too. For some reason, her day had seemed like a week.

"Well, maybe I ought to go to the country club now and see if I can get ahold of Bruce," Ken stood up and leaned down and gave Danika a quick kiss on the cheek. "Your face looks like hell," he smiled as he straightened back up.

"So I've been told," Danika replied and nodded her head as Ken left the room.

"Thanks for the flowers!" she yelled as he disappeared down the hall. But it was too late. He was gone and for some reason she couldn't help but feel that the conversation seemed strained between them today. Maybe he wasn't wanting to get back into her life again after all?

CHAPTER SIXTEEN

Danika put in a rough night. Every part of her body hurt. Her head, her neck, her back, her skin! Her legs and feet were a dumb numb hurt and felt totally different than the rest of her aching parts. The shots of Demerol only lasted for a couple of hours and then the pain would start creeping back in, and by the time four hours rolled around so she could have another shot, she would be in tears from the pain. Maybe if she had something to do besides just lying there and feeling sorry for herself, she wouldn't notice it so much. But, it seemed the more she tried to think of something besides herself, the memories of the past two days would start playing havoc with her mind again. How long would she have to be like this?

Finally she could see the first rays of sunshine start to peek into the window of her room, and before long the clattering noises of the first shift crew coming on board were eminent. Hopefully today she would know for sure what was going to take place as far as her body was concerned, and maybe, just maybe, they might even let her have another cup of that hot tasty coffee. But what she was looking forward to the most was seeing Jani again. She hadn't seen her since last Thanksgiving when they had come back to Iowa for four days to spend with her and Ken. They had spent Christmas with Rick's family in Wisconsin.

And now as Danika thought about it, she vaguely remembered Jani talking about Rick's sister having a new baby and how she couldn't wait for them to start raising a family. But, Danika had been so busy fixing a special lunch for Rick and Jani that she had just passed it off by telling Jani to not rush things. And that was the last that anything had been said about having a new baby. Now she wished she would have paid more attention to what Jani was talking about. But as usual, Danika was in one of her busy, busy moods and didn't pay attention like she should have.

Tears started trickling down the sides of her cheeks again as she thought back about so many times that she had been too busy to pay attention to her daughter like she should have been, and now look at what it had gotten her. She was a lonely woman and things weren't looking good. She had no one to depend on for security. Her mother's life depended on Danika for her care and needs. But, Danika had no one but herself. Jani couldn't leave her home or her life with a loving husband and a new baby just to worry about or to take care of her.

"Good morning!" A young nurse's aide entered the room carrying a pile of fresh bedding and a clean hospital gown. "Would you like a quick bath before the day starts?" she asked sweetly.

"I would love to take a shower!" Danika eagerly replied.

"I'm sorry, but not yet! You have to just take it easy and stay flat on your back for a couple more days. I will give you a sponge bath and that should make you feel better."

Danika couldn't remember ever having someone besides Ken give her a scrub down. And that had always been a most pleasurable experience in a hot steamy bath tub. She was certain this wouldn't be near as exciting as those baths with him had been.

"So tell me what I'm supposed to do."

The young aide just smiled, pulled the curtain around the bed so no one could see what she was about to do, and said, "You just lay there and enjoy it, and I will do the rest."

All kinds of thoughts ran through Danika's head and they weren't good. But, it actually felt good as the aide used steaming hot water out of a wash basin and lathered up Danika's body, including her pits and privates, and rinsed her thoroughly with more hot steamy water. She let Danika wash her own face and then worked a dry foam into her hair to get any blood or dirt out of it. By the time it was all over and she had put a clean gown on Danika, much to Danika's surprise, she felt like a different person, and she thought she even was experiencing less pain than earlier. She was even surprised at how efficiently the aide was able to put clean bedding on the bed with Danika still in it.

The aide handed Danika a mirror so she could see how her face looked, and Danika gasped. Was it any wonder that Ken didn't give her a nice juicy kiss when he was there? Her face was a big lumpy mess of reddish blue bruises and dark purple circles surrounding each eye. Surprisingly, her nose was still intact and wasn't crooked, so therefore, even though it hurt to touch it, it hadn't been broken. That was a big relief.

The aide had just left the room when an older woman came bringing in a breakfast tray with a hot cup of coffee on it, plus a glass of apple juice and a couple pieces of toast. "I'm sorry you can't have a heavier breakfast, but Doctor ordered a light breakfast until we get all the results of your tests back," the woman apologized.

"Right now I feel like this is a meal fit for a queen," Danika laughed. "I can't wait to sip that coffee!"

The woman looked pleased with Danika's answer and left the room. And before Danika could even tip the straw to the steaming brew to her lips, Beau walked into the room.

"Well, you look cheerful this morning. Are you feeling better?"

"I do feel a little bit better this morning," Danika grinned. "What brings you here so early?"

"I wasn't sure what all they had planned for you today, so I was hoping I could get a statement from you right away."

"Oh!" Danika felt that zing of disappointment again when she realized that the only reason he was there was to do his job and not necessarily to see her again.

"What do you need to know?"

"Everything that happened from the time you left your apartment until the time that our agents were able to rescue you."

Danika scowled, "Did you rescue me or did I rescue myself?"

"I would like to think that maybe I had a little something to do with it," he grinned.

"Yes, I'm sure you did, and I appreciate it," Danika smiled.

She took another swallow of the hot coffee, wishing that she could consume all of it, plus the toast before it got cold, but oh well! It was going to be a challenge to learn how to eat while she was lying flat on her back, anyway. And he was the last person she wanted to see her first try at it.

He sat down in the chair next to her bed and pulled a wireless h/p tablet out of his brief case before she started telling him her long horrible tale. Twice he stopped her when she told why she had been abducted.

"Diamonds?"

"Yes! He kept accusing me of having the diamonds that Marty had stolen from him over the weekend. He said Marty had killed his van driver and stolen the diamonds."

"Did he say where the diamonds were being transported from?"

Danika shook her head.

Beau scratched his chin and said, "That explains a few things. But what made him think you had them?"

"Marty told him that he had placed them in my tote bag at the restaurant after he knocked me down."

"Wait! I'm confused! Why would Marty knock you down and put the stolen diamonds in your tote bag?"

"I don't know!" Danika exclaimed. "I just know that Emanuel sent his men to find them in my apartment and when they didn't find them, he sent them on to my office to look for them. I think his men stole them and my diamond ring and just didn't want Emanuel to know about it."

Beau looked extremely puzzled. "Something about all of this isn't making sense! Did Marty get a chance to tell you why he picked you?"

Danika shook her head. "He was beaten so bad by the time I was put in the room with him, that he could barely talk. It was awful!"

"Who was with you at the restaurant?"

Danika shrugged her shoulders. "Just Ken! And he was really upset when Marty knocked me into the fig tree."

Once more Beau looked puzzled and shook his head. "Okay, go on. Finish telling me how and why you were driving the car and why you crashed it through the gate like you did."

So Danika proceeded to finish her story, and when she was done, Beau stood up and squeezed her hand. "I'm so glad you are still here to tell your story." His smile was tender and almost wistful.

"So am I or else you wouldn't be able to know what all Emanuel and Marty were up to," Danika replied.

Beau frowned. "That's not the only reason. I'm thankful you weren't hurt worse."

"We don't know yet how bad it is," Danika stated. "Right now I don't have any feeling in my legs or feet." Those damned tears welled up in her eyes again and she couldn't stop them.

Beau sat back down in the chair. "Why didn't you tell me this yesterday?"

"You didn't ask!" she replied.

"I'm so sorry! What are they saying about it?"

Danika told him what she knew and wiped the tears away with a tissue.

He sat there without saying anything and Danika was so choked up that she couldn't say anything either. He squeezed her hand tighter and just as he stood up, Ken and Jani walked into the room.

"Since when did special FBI agents need to give hands on care to their victims?" Ken snarled.

"FBI agents check in on their special victims all the time," Beau answered. "Especially when they need statements from them! And as a matter of fact, you are on my list to visit yet today to retrieve a statement from too."

"Why me?" Ken scowled. "I don't know anything about stolen diamonds."

"Who said anything about stolen diamonds?" Beau asked.

"I…, you…!" Ken's face turned red. 'I'm sure Dani mentioned them when she was telling me all about what happened to her and Marty Vineteri."

Beau turned and looked at Danika, and she nodded her head.

"Well, I don't know anything about stolen diamonds, nor do I care," Jani grinned. "I just care about my mother. So if you men will excuse us, she and I have a lot of catching up to do!" With those words, she hurried across the room and gathered Danika into her arms like a mother does a small child.

Beau smiled at Danika and said, "I assume this is the daughter that is about to give you your first grandchild?"

"You assumed right," Danika answered through the rash of those endless tears that she had shed so much of the past couple of days and had absolutely no control over.

"Well, thanks, Danika," Beau gave her another ardent smile, "I will get this printed up and then bring it back for you to read and sign if you agree."

Danika nodded.

"I will catch up to you later," Beau said to Ken as he passed by him on his way out the door.

"What makes him think I have anything to do with the missing diamonds?" Ken frowned at Danika. "What all did you tell him?"

"I just told him how Marty had bumped into me at the restaurant, and had told Emanuel that he put the diamonds in my tote bag that day as he helped me up. That's all!"

Danika turned her attention away from Ken and back to Jani, but not before she noticed the odd look on Ken's face when he ran his hand over his chin as if in deep thought about something.

Jani spent the day at the hospital with Danika while Ken returned to his office. She was so excited about her new baby girl coming that before Danika knew what was happening, she was sharing that excitement too. They discussed names and all the things that Danika thought Jani would need for a nursery. They both agreed on a white French provincial style crib and bassinet, plus a chest of drawers to match. And then they discussed what the designs in the room should be. Jani said her and Rick couldn't agree on the theme, so what did her mother like? It brought back so many wonderful memories of when Danika had decorated Jani's nursery, and before long, she was coming up with all kinds of great ideas that pleased Jani.

"Oh Mom! I can't wait for you to come and see our new house!" Jani exclaimed. "I want you to come just as soon as you feel up to it so we can go shopping for it and the nursery."

"You didn't tell me that you were in the process of purchasing a new home," Danika frowned.

"I thought I told you!" Jani said.

"No..., you said you couldn't afford one like you wanted."

"Well, we found the perfect home, and Dad gave us the twenty five thousand dollars that we needed for the down payment. We get to close the deal the first of the month, so we will get to move shortly after that just as soon as we get it redecorated."

"How are you going to redecorate?" Danika couldn't help but feel and sound skeptical.

"I know I'm always asking you for money, but this time we have saved enough that you won't have to help us. I just want you to come and give me ideas. You have seen so many different ideas during your lifetime, so I was hoping you could give me some suggestions."

Jani seemed so excited over all the great new things that was taking place in her life, that Danika didn't have the heart to disagree with her on any issue.

"Besides," Jani beamed. "I'm sure that if we need any more money for our house, Dad will be willing to help us out. You had to pay for everything while I was growing up and he said that now it was his turn to help us out."

"That was nice of him," Danika replied in a repugnant tone.

"Oh Mom! Don't be so hard on him. He knows he made a mistake."

"And just where did your dad get all this money that he is going to help you with?" Danika asked, while trying to sweeten her attitude a little bit.

"I don't know! I just know he said he had come into a windfall, so he could help us out with anything we needed.

"Well Honey, I'm not sure when I will be out of the hospital or even how much good I can be to you," Danika confessed. "Did your dad tell you that right now I don't have any feeling in my legs?"

"Yes, but he also said you didn't know yet!"

"True! But it sounds like I might be in here for a while even if the feeling starts coming back. That young good looking Dr. Sheppard said for me to plan on at least ten days and possibly more if I have to do physical therapy.

"Don't worry," Jani laughed. "The baby isn't due for another five months. So just as soon as you are done with therapy you can come and stay with us to recoup."

"What if I'm in a wheelchair?"

"We will cross that bridge when we get to it! You always taught me that nothing was too high or too tough to prevent a person from accomplishing something if they really wanted to do it. And you've always been my inspiration to accomplish everything that I wanted to do. You sat the example for me."

Danika lost it again! The tears rushed harder than ever down her cheeks when she heard the words that Jani had just said to her.

"I didn't feel like I sat a very good example," she wailed. "I lost everything that really mattered when your dad and I got a divorce and I no longer had you under my wing. All the money in the world can't buy love and happiness. And now look what it bought me! Possibly a wheelchair for the rest of my life!"

Jani hugged her mom again and together they shed an overabundance of tears.

"Am I interrupting a family reunion?" Dr. Sheppard asked.

Wiping her tears as best she could, Danika said, "Dr. Sheppard, this is my daughter from Colorado and she just flew in this morning to spend some time with me."

"Good!" The doctor extended his hand to Jani and said, "Well, Ms. Bronson, I have some great news for you. The MRI doesn't show any damaged nerves in your spine, so I'm sure that just as soon as the swelling goes down around your fractured vertebras, you should start getting the feeling back into your legs and feet."

"Mom! That's wonderful news!" Jani exclaimed.

"So! When can I take a shower and get a decent meal?" Danika asked.

"The decent meal you can have tonight and the shower not so fast. We will talk about that in a couple of more days," Dr. Sheppard laughed.

"She has to hurry up and get to walking again, because she has to help me design a new nursery!" Jani explained.

"Are you going to be a grandmother?" Dr. Sheppard asked Danika.

""Yes! And our little girl is supposed to be born on my birthday!" Danika gleamed.

"Is this your first?" he asked.

"Yes!"

"That is great news!" Dr. Sheppard grinned. "In that case, we will try extra hard to get you back on your feet. They tell me that there is nothing more exciting than becoming a grandparent."

"I guess I'm about to find out," Danika laughed.

After Dr. Sheppard left the room, Jani giggled and said, "You were right, Mom! He really *is* good looking. I would recuperate real fast if I had him taking care of me."

""Yes, but…, the faster I recuperate, the less time I can enjoy looking at him," Danika giggled too.

Jani stayed until her dad came to pick her up after he got off work, and Danika had thoroughly enjoyed the day, just spending time with her. It was something that they hadn't done since they had spent time together shopping for Jani's big wedding day. When Jani was a teenager, she spent some of her weekends with Danika, but so often she had plans with friends or activities, so she was off doing her own thing. But Danika had cherished the days that they had to go shopping or just doing so many things that girls do on a girls' day out. Since Jani had gotten married and moved to Denver, they no longer had those days together, and Danika hadn't realized how much she had missed them until right now.

CHAPTER SEVENTEEN

Jani and Ken had just left to go get something to eat when Tara and Josh walked into Danika's room with more flowers. Danika was more than surprised and absolutely pleased to see them.

"How did you know that I was in here?" she asked.

"When I kept trying to call your cell phone and it continuously went into voicemail, I knew something had to be wrong. So, I took a chance and called the district attorney's office, and since your Ex was in court today, the office girl told me what I wanted to know. And then at noon, your Ex called me back and told me more details, plus who your insurance agent was.

"Why did you need the name of my insurance agent?" Danika asked.

"Well, all of your employees have decided that just as soon as the insurance settlement comes through, they want to come in and clean it up and get it back into shape so they can start working again. Unemployment will help them until they can get it going again. But it can't be a permanent thing to try to live off of. And the insurance man and your husband both think that since it was an act of criminal mischief and the perpetrator has been caught, that your claim shouldn't take too long to come through. In the meantime, we can go ahead and get started cleaning it up on our own time. Which, we have a lot of right now!"

Danika had never been at such a loss of words as she was right now. What did you say to something such as this? And once more, that plague of tears started rushing down her cheeks. She had never cried as much in her entire lifetime as she had in the past few days and that in itself was completely maddening.

"Who is going to go ahead with it?" Danika finally was able to clear her throat enough to talk.

"Josh and I will!" Tara answered. "We pretty much know everything that we need and how to make it work."

"And now that we know where you are, we can always ask you to guide us through what we aren't sure about," Josh grinned. "Tara can take care of all the red tape work that is needed and I can take care of the crew."

Danika just started laughing. "What if I don't get to come back for a while?"

"We will handle it," Josh said. "Besides, everyone wants their job back. They know what they are supposed to be doing to keep it going, plus what has to be done to make it work."

"Anything that has to be signed by you can be done right here in this hospital room," Tara explained. "We will even bring your laptop in to you so you can keep up with us through skype."

"I don't have a laptop any more. It was stolen the night my apartment was broken into."

"Then we will get you a new one. I can pretty much download everything off of my computer on to it that you will need," Tara smiled. "Was the company bank account on that laptop?"

"Tara, you are a life saver!" Danika declared.

"Me?" Tara laughed. "How am I a lifesaver?"

"I forgot all about my bank account records being on the laptop. I need to call the bank right away and put a stop on everything and open a different account for you to work with. Did they take the company checkbook?"

"No! Thank goodness!" Tara replied. "Was your account password protected?"

"Yes."

"Let's hope whoever has the laptop hasn't figured out the password yet."

Danika nodded her head, and said, "It looks like you two have it all thought out! What is there for me to argue with?"

"Absolutely nothing!" Tara answered. "We just want you to concentrate on getting better."

"I doesn't sound like I have a choice, do I?"

"Nope!" Josh and Tara said in unison.

They spent a few more minutes asking Danika more questions about what all she had been through before Danika's dinner tray of baked chicken breast, rice pilaf and a fruit salad arrived, and then they decided to leave.

Danika looked at the tray sitting on the bedside table and wondered how she was supposed to eat it or even be able to get to it while she was lying flat on her back. She had just squeezed the call light button and asked for help when Beau walked through the door, and he was dressed in a Polo shirt and dress pants again, looking sexier than ever. And when he approached her bed he had on that same fragranced cologne that he had worn just a few nights before. She had to fight the uncontrollable urge to just yank him into her bed so she could wrap herself around him and indulge in the same exhilarating experience that they had shared that awesome night.

"You called, Madam?" he grinned.

"I don't remember asking for you!" Danika answered.

"Well, you have me. What can I help you with?"

"I'm not sure how I'm supposed to be able to cut up meat and eat while I'm lying flat like this."

"I can feed you."

Danika started laughing.

"What! I was a good dad and learned the hard way how to feed wiggling, spitting, little people. You aren't going to wiggle and spit at me, are you?"

"No," Danika laughed even harder.

"Okay then! I am going to feed you. But first, I have something for you."

"What is it?" Danika asked. "I like surprises."

He reached in his back pants pocket and pulled out her cell phone. "I thought maybe you could use this while you are just laying here thinking of something to do."

"Where did you find it?"

"My crew found it in the office of Emanuel's house when they were searching it. They also found Marty Vineteri's phone, and we hope to find some pretty interesting stuff on it."

"Like what?"

"Well, I'm not at liberty to tell you, but I have a feeling that his phone is going to tell us who stole your jewelry box, laptop, and Emanuel's diamonds."

"How long are you going to keep me in suspense?"

"Long enough for you to eat your dinner," he laughed.

With that, he picked the fork up off of the tray and scooped up a bite of rice for her. But when he got it almost to her mouth, the rice slipped off the fork and spilled on her chin and all over her neck. They both started laughing and he said, "I guess it's been a few days since I tried feeding someone!" He jumped up and grabbed a couple of paper towels out of the bathroom and began cleaning the rice off of her face and throat. All she could do was laugh. And, it seemed so good to be laughing with someone after all the doom that had happened in the past few days.

After he finished cleaning the rice off of her neck, he cut up her chicken and said, "I think we will just stick to something that I am sure won't fall off all over you." And so it went. He fed her the chicken and fresh fruit salad, and when she asked for it, he held the cup of now tepid coffee so she could drink it through the straw.

When he had finished feeding her, he slid the tray table to the side, and pulled his chair around so he was close to her bedside and could look directly at her.

"So now, are you going to tell me what was on Marty's phone?" Danika asked.

"I said, I thought maybe it would tell us what we needed to know. I didn't say that it did for sure, did I?"

"No," Danika grinned. "So may I ask what brought you here this evening? I know you didn't come just to feed me!"

"Yes I did! I came just to see you and see what I could do to help."

Their eyes connected in a manner in which they never had before, and Danika felt those butterflies fluttering inside. She was afraid to even speak because she felt so much like a giddish school girl right now that she just knew whatever she attempted to say would come out over the lips all wrong.

Evidently, he was feeling the same thing because they both seemed to be at a loss of words. Finally he reached over and took ahold of her hand and squeezed it.

"It's good to see you smile," he whispered.

"Thank you." And after that they just sat a few seconds absorbing the moment before she spoke again.

"If you want to help, could you please see if my two bank accounts have been jeopardized? I need to close them both before the pervert hacks in and figures out my passwords. Tara will be able to give you the business account numbers, and I don't remember if my personal checks were stolen out of my desk or not. Can you please check on it for me?"

"Yes," he agreed. "I will see what I can do. I may need to get a search warrant before they will give me that information."

"Whatever it takes, please do it."

"Well, if it makes you feel any better, I believe Emanuel when he states that his men didn't steal your laptop and jewelry box. He swears that they only had orders to find the diamonds and nothing else. He admitted to his men shooting the security guard and doing the damage at your office after they couldn't find the stones at your apartment."

"And what makes you believe him?"

"He swears he and his chauffeur were sitting outside in the parking lot of your apartment while two of his men tore the place up. He would have seen them carry out the laptop and jewelry box if they had it."

Beau stayed for at least an hour longer and he and Danika talked more about what had happened and how so far everything was up in the air while investigators worked at trying to find some good solid forensics. He was sure it would just be a matter of time before they had some answers that would lead to issuing several arrests and charges being made. After he left, Danika had a chance to just lay and think about some things.

So many things started running back through her head, and it bothered her that she had told Ken as much as she had. Of course, if she couldn't trust him, who could she trust? But one of the things that kept flashing back through her mind was, the look on Ken's face after Beau told him that he was going to give him a visit. And then more flashes seeped in. Why did Marty pick her tote bag to put diamonds in? There were plenty of other people there that he could have slipped them to. But he picked her. And how did he or whoever stole them know where she lived so they could retrieve them? She thought about how he had constantly watched her while they were eating. Did he, or did he not know she was behind him when he whirled around and knocked her over? And still another thought crossed her mind. Ken had mentioned that they go to McDonald's for breakfast until he received a phone call. And when he got off the phone, he changed his mind and suggested Perkins instead. Why? And why didn't it strike her as odd at the time?

But still, she remembered how Ken had come through the door and confronted Marty after he had knocked her over. And hadn't he warned her about what could happen? But that was about the article. Not about any missing diamonds.

The article! She had almost completely forgotten about the magazine article! How did any of this tie in together? Danika couldn't wait for Beau to come up with some answers. And come to think about it, she didn't remember telling Ken that the diamonds were stolen. She had just told him that Emanuel had abducted her because he thought she had his diamonds.

Danika couldn't get to sleep after that. All she could think about was the flashbacks that had been pouring through her head all night after Beau had left. She had just dozed partially off to sleep when another thought hit her hard. And it hit her too hard for comfort and the pain was becoming stronger with each breathing moment. Jani said her dad was giving them the money they needed for a down payment on a house because he had recently came into a windfall. Where did that windfall come from all of a sudden?

She had to get ahold of Beau! But how? She didn't have his phone number. And suddenly, she didn't feel safe.

CHAPTER EIGHTEEN

Danika was struggling at trying to drink her coffee through a straw and eating a piece of toast off of her breakfast tray when Ken and Jani walked in. She knew the thoughts that had been running through her head all night were standing on top of her chest just waiting to shout at Ken with all kinds of accusations and questions. She had trouble disguising a fake cheery "good morning" when they walked in.

"Well, you look better this morning," Ken smiled. "You must have gotten a good night's rest."

"I think so," Danika replied. "Did you two have a good visit?"

"Yes!" Jani spoke up. "We discussed some of the same things that you and I talked about yesterday."

"Like what?" Danika asked.

"Oh…, things like when we could close the deal on our house and things like that," Jani said.

"I'm sorry! I forget when you said you were going to take possession," Danika tried casting a sweet smile.

"Well…," Jani glanced up at her dad. "We may have to wait another month. Some unforeseen things have come up."

"Over night?" Danika was surprised. "What could possibly come up to cancel the deal over night?"

Ken cleared his throat and said, "I will leave you two so you can visit and then I'll be back to pick you up at ten so you can catch your plane."

"What?" Danika scowled at Jani. "Don't tell me you are leaving so soon?"

"Yes, I'm afraid I have to. I need to get home and talk to Rick about some things."

"I'm sorry to hear that, Honey," Danika stated. "It seems like I just don't get to see enough of you when you come to Iowa."

But Ken didn't get to leave. Not at the present time, anyway, because Beau and a couple of police officers walked into Danika's room.

"What is this all about?" Ken frowned.

"Kenneth Bronson, these police officers are here to arrest you for the destruction of Danika Bronson's property and the theft of several of her valuable items. I am here to arrest you for stealing illegal black market diamonds and transporting them across state lines. You have the right to remain silent. Anything you say may be used against you in a court of law."

"I know what my rights are," Ken growled.

"Daddy! What is he talking about?" Jani started screaming. "What did you do?"

"I'm sorry, Honey," his face had turned an ashen gray. "I was so tired of your mother always giving you what you needed and me never able to help you. I knew how disappointed you were that you didn't have the money to buy the house that you wanted and when you said you hated to ask your mother for it, I decided I was going to do something worthwhile for a change. I had a chance to make $100,000 by making a deal with the mafia and turning my head away from charges that should have been brought against them. All I had to do was find a way for Marty to steal Vasquez's diamonds when they came into town."

Ken looked at Danika and said, "I'm sorry, Sweetheart. You weren't supposed to get caught in the middle of it. I didn't realize Vasquez would go so far to try finding them."

Jani broke down and started crying at the same time that Danika watched in horror at the police leading Ken out of the hospital. What had he done?

Beau put his arm around Jani and said, "I'm sorry this had to happen to both you and your mother. I didn't have any other alternative besides this to take."

"How did you know?" Danika asked.

"I told you Marty's cell phone would give us the answers. And it did."

"Did it tell you where my laptop and jewelry box went?"

"No, but I have a feeling that Ken will be willing to tell us that. It seems the mafia lord had sent a couple of their thugs in to your apartment to get the diamonds and the jewelry box as well as the laptop. Ken asked them to. He knew how much the ring was worth, and he also wanted access to your banking account. They must have been in and out right before Vasquez's men got there."

"I can't believe my dad would do something like that," Jani was wailing.

"People will do funny things sometimes when they are desperate," Beau replied.

"What did he tell you about the loan for your house?" Danika asked.

"He just told me last night that he had run into a snag getting that windfall he was expecting, and that it would only be a few more days before it came through. I never dreamed the windfall was something illegal. After all these years of him being the most wonderful dad a girl could ask for."

"Don't forget that either, Jani, as long as you live," Danika said. "He is still a wonderful Dad and always will be. He did this for you. He has always been there for you when I wasn't. Now it's my turn to be there for you. And I will be. I'll see to it that you get the money for your house. Besides, I have to have a room to stay in when my new granddaughter comes. I want to take my turn at walking the floor with her, too."

Beau leaned down and pinched Danika's toe and said, "That bedroom has to be big enough for both of us."

Danika started screaming, startling both Beau and Jani. "Pinch my toe again! I felt it! Do it again and again to all of my toes to make sure I'm not dreaming and actually have feeling in all of them."

And then she stopped and asked, "What do you mean the bedroom has to be big enough for both of us?"

"Yes! What do you mean?" Jani asked.

"I don't know for sure when that new baby is coming, but I know your mother and I are going to have a honeymoon just as soon as she gets released from this hospital," Beau grinned.

"Mom! You didn't tell me you were getting married!"

"I didn't know it either, but I'm sure not going to argue with it!" Danika laughed. And then she added, "Beau even knows how to feed wiggly, spitting babies."

"And change diapers. Don't forget that!" he chimed in.

"Oh we won't," Jani giggled. "Maybe this bitter sweet day hasn't turned out so bad after all."

THE END

OTHER BOOKS PUBLISHED BY SANDI LORRAINE:

The Escape

Love's Enduring Choices

A Winter to Remember

Heartache vs Heartbreak

Finding Hope

Is It Revenge?

One Last Chance

Printed in the United States
By Bookmasters